Mrs. Frederick pushes her bifocals onto her nose and scans her roster. "We're going to do this alphabetically, so when I call your names, go sit with your partner."

Chase Dobbs's eyes slide over to Benjie Durbin. *Oh please, Lord, unite me and Benjie. Granted, he's fifteen and still jokes about farting and bras, but I love him. I do. He got every science award there was last term.*

He's halfway across the room when the door opens. And there she is, in a wool mulberry cape, black racing gloves, her cheeks pinked by cold and her flat chest heaving.

Frederick says, "Chase, you need to move back to your desk, and Parker, you're going to be his lab partner."

Parker smiles shyly at Chase, who dies a bloody death inside.

DON'T MISS A SEMESTER . . .

The Upper Class

Miss Educated:
An Upper Class Novel

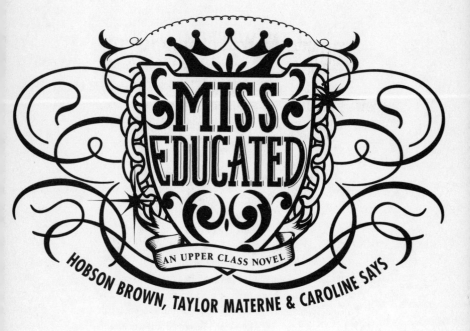

MISS EDUCATED

AN UPPER CLASS NOVEL

HOBSON BROWN, TAYLOR MATERNE & CAROLINE SAYS

HARPER TEEN

An Imprint of HarperCollins*Publishers*

ACKNOWLEDGMENTS

The authors would like to thank Sally Wofford-Girand, their agent, and Amanda Maciel, their editor. In addition, Caroline Says would like to thank The Edward F. Albee Foundation, The Ucross Foundation, The Constance Saltonstall Foundation, and Ledig House.

HarperTeen is an imprint of
HarperCollins Publishers.

Library of Congress Catalog Card Number: 2007925199
ISBN 978-0-06-085083-8

Typography by Jennifer Heuer
❖
First Edition

This book is for our friends.

1

Parker and Blue mosey down the hair-product aisle of Shoppers Drug Mart, the Canadian January sky distilled into a creamy gray. Parker's leaving tomorrow, and she gets butterflies each time her mind even grazes Wellington and the new semester.

She's looking at Blue, her best friend at home, as if for the first time. He's only five two, and looks like he'll stay that way. He wears liner around crazy-looking blue eyes and jacks up his black hair so he resembles a terrier. His wide-legged black pants drag on the linoleum floor, collecting dust bunnies. She imagines him at Wellington. *Would he even get past the gates?*

"Hmmm," he says, scanning the shelf.

"There," Parker says, pointing.

"No, that's not it. They said it's in a red container."

They're looking for violet-scented pomade, which some-one told Blue about, and he wants it for a Baudelaire party later this week.

"I've used this one; I like it," he says, pointing a plat-form-shoe toe at a glittery gel on the bottom rack.

"I bet you got sparkles all over your pillowcase, though," she says, and he laughs.

Blue laughs more than most people. He's got experience crammed into his pint-sized self, years of foster care, years of seeing and hearing things most kids don't know about. He's not sure who his parents are, or if he's part Japanese or Mexican or something else; people often study him and try to guess his origins. He swears that he won't live past thirty, that he doesn't want to. Blue says: *Live like you mean it.*

"I'm going to have to go to that beauty shop on Willowbay," he says in defeat as they pass through auto-matic doors. "Those pissers, they lied to me; they said it was here."

"It's a conspiracy, Blue, to keep you from your rightful hairdo."

"Shut it, beauty queen."

"What does that mean?" she asks, hurt.

"You're getting beautiful." He speaks without looking at her, unchaining his bike from the rail. And that's how she knows he means it.

"God, it's weird," he says, still without glancing at her. "When you left this fall, it seemed like a trial or something. Like we would get you back. Now it feels real. Like you belong to them, to that place."

Parker throws her arm around Blue, squeezes him. They stand in the cold lot. She can't confirm or deny what he's saying, because she knows she belongs, at this point, to both places and so, in a sense, to neither in full. "You're going to make me cry, Blue."

"Don't do that." Then he pushes her away, and she pushes him back, and they laugh.

They get on their dirt bikes. Parker in black-and-white Adidas high-tops with the gold tongue, and a raccoon coat she found in her basement. Blue with no jacket and no hat, just I Ching cards stuck into the spokes of his wheel. They ride, speeding and skittering on the icy shoulder of the highway, occasionally letting out a full-moon howl for the hell of it. Dangerous, and alive.

2

Chase stamps his feet on the cement walk outside the deserted Connecticut airport. He takes a drag and exhales upward to watch the smoke billow in the hard, starry, northeast night.

"Holy shit!" he says again, having already said it a few times. He's just having trouble processing the bitch-slap of icy wind he received stepping through those lonely glass doors to smoke.

But he'd rather freeze his ass off to kill this crumpled soft-pack than wait inside. His flight from Charleston to New York had been on time, but then he was delayed from LaGuardia to Hartford, and Chase missed the school shuttle. Only fourteen hours ago, he was sitting on the river in a flats boat, the birdsong in the South Carolina woods atonal, haunting as church bells. His father's monstrous red knuckles had flexed as he reeled in his line, a cap on his big head, white hair sticking in tufts from the sides. The lecture Chase got was like fire in his ears.

Chase sparks another Red.

I must pull it together this semester. No dicking around. A pint of Stoli hangs heavily in the pocket of his camelhair coat— he'd meant to douse his tomato juice on the plane, but the stewardess hovered, and the businessman in the next seat seemed to be minus a sense of humor. So he takes a mean, lukewarm sip now and chucks the pint in the garbage can. *Get rid of it.*

His father had dropped the bomb. If Wellington doesn't work, it's military school, where his father is on the board. Not up for discussion. Chase barely passed his first semester, and his teachers, his advisor, and his floormaster called over the holidays to let the family know Chase was walking a tightrope.

Man, warm vodka tastes like hell.

His father's words echo like wind chimes through the barren clouds. "Grow up, son."

A maroon Chevy with *Glendon Taxi* scripted in baby blue on its side jerks and stutters up to the curb. Chase throws his luggage in the trunk.

"Hello there—" Chase falters, wanting to add *Sir* or *Ma'am* but not sure if the white-haired pompadoured sourpuss is male or female. "I'm, uh, I'm going–"

"I know where you're going," the driver croaks in condemnation, his or her eyeballs sliding to take a quick look at the passenger before the cab squeals onto the ghostly pavement.

They drive on roads that aren't country lanes but aren't highways. Winter has been steadily stripping Connecticut of life, and Chase surveys its work: a now brittle, skeletal topography. He muses on what he's just left, a city that in January isn't warm but isn't cold, just wet and quiet. At home the magnolia leaves were elegant, glossy, and dark green, the branches promising a perfumed white springtime soon enough. He thinks of his mom's stone-ground grits, creamy and steaming, her blue-cheese coleslaw, the boiled peanuts bloated in their shells. A mahogany bed with down pillows. Rain dripping off porticos.

"Can I smoke in here?" he asks.

"I don't care *what* you do" is how the creature in the front says *yes*.

Chase cracks the filthy window and lights his last cigarette, his lucky. Cold air rushes in the sliver of open window. Hissing through the radio static is a Bon Jovi song.

Vacation is over. Chase is heading back to school empty-handed, no liquor or cigarettes secreted away in his bags. He just got a new asshole torn by his dad. So why, as the land converges to become familiar, and the car's lights burn a hole into the trees near campus, why does he feel a thrill? What is he racing back for?

The grounds are phosphorescent with snow, cornices and eaves gleaming in the after-check-in hush. And here's Chase, starting off the term late for curfew—but Continental goddamn Airlines will have to take the fall for this one.

Anyone seeing him walk up to the old building could think it's 1969. Chase is on that cusp of disenchantment that was stylish then. Like a reluctant movie star who hangs out with Pete Fonda and Dennis Hopper, he's got leftover pretty-boy in him, and a disillusioned renegade coming up in his soul like a tiger. His hair is long, almost to his shoulders, parted in the middle—it's the red flag he waves in the face of his bullish father.

Mr. Dobbs says over and over: *Shouldn't I be the one out of date here? Shouldn't* you *be trying to get it through to* me *that it's the twenty-first century? Christ, boy, where's the draft-card-burning party tonight?*

Chase always answers: *This isn't a political statement, Dad.*

Even worse! his father replies, because his father never fails to reply. *I would be ecstatic if you could empty your pockets and show me some convictions, son. Stand up for something, goddamnit.*

But the girls at Wellington like his look. Chase knows

his effect on people to some extent, he just doesn't realize that it's widespread. His Facebook pic is taped to the walls of Prep girls' corkboards, circled with a red heart. He's the up-and-coming rock star of the school.

Shouldering his duffel now, he crunches across the snow to Cadwallader's door, and the sound echoes in the black sky. He enters the dorm, and although the first-floor doors are shut there's a buzz of guys talking, ridiculing, laughing, and bragging. Snow melts off his shoes as he clomps up stone stairs. And here's his crew.

Slumped on the hallway floor, eating popcorn and drinking Gatorade—Greg, Gabriel, Burns, and Noah. They smile slowly, stand up to high-five. Greg flickers, that way he does, with cold, mean cynicism, and then with warmth, his long, girlish lashes batting over his brown eyes. He slouches, athletic, the power of his muscles dormant but evident. Noah's brought the city with him, the way guests drag cold winter air into your home from outside on their clothes. Gabriel's accent is stronger, having been renewed for a month in Colombia. His long-sleeved white Lacoste shirt tucked into black jeans, in a way no American kid would wear it. And his body language reveals signs of being spoiled and also goaded into growing up; his parents are training him for a future Chase can't fathom.

And there's Burns. With dishwater hair too long for a crew cut and too short to comb down, it stands on his head like Pomeranian fur. He's got the pink and wrinkled appeal of a newborn hamster. His parents are grandparent age, and his nanny has always dressed him. As usual he's in an idiosyncratic outfit: a tracksuit jacket and khakis.

"Where you been, brother?" Noah says.

"Thought you went AWOL," Greg chides.

"Well, I spent some quality time in LaGuardia, reading *Penthouse* and eating Burger King," Chase says.

"Hell, you should've got soused, dude." Burns pouts.

Chase smiles at the attention. But he's already feeling lame about his new good-behavior goals. Can these guys understand the wrath and power of Mr. Randall Dobbs: Vietnam vet, Marine, Southern gentleman, aristocrat, esteemed businessman? Keeper of Chase's destiny?

But can any son explain his father? Chase isn't sure. He only knows that for him it isn't just about being grounded or getting yelled at. It's a much more profound phenomenon. His father is as big as the sun, and when he's shining on you, all is good. His brother, Reed, spends most of his time in the sun. Chase spends a lot of time in the dark, walking, trembling with cold, trying to appear blasé and comfortable to any onlookers.

"You *do* smell like an ashtray, man," Burns continues, sniffing Chase like a dog, his scrawny nose wrinkling with pleasure.

"Thank you," Chase says sincerely, enjoying his own

acrid, burned, sweet smell—strongest on the fingers of his left hand.

"Why don't we burn one down in the bathroom, welcome-back-style," Noah suggests, lounging laconically against the cinder block wall.

And there it is. Chase teeters between going with the flow, which is his favorite pastime, and spilling the beans on his academic probation and subsequent paternal probation. Chase hates being left out. When he knows people are hanging out and misbehaving without him, his stomach burns with something like anger or anxiety, but it's neither. It's the sensation a dumb animal gets when it wakes up and smells that its herd has wandered a few miles away.

"I don't know," Chase hedges.

"What's the hang up?" Noah asks.

He still has to call his parents to let them know he got here safely. This is enough, for now, to keep him straight and narrow. Some men can sip wine and pick out notes of vanilla, tobacco, peach; Mr. Dobbs can speak to his son on a telephone and smell whiffs of Parliaments, Southern Comfort, Skoal.

So he chooses to be elusive. "Christ, I smoked two packs of Reds to the filter en route, my friends. I'll projectile vomit if I have another one."

Noah turns to Greg. "How about you?"

"Maybe in a minute, man."

So the idea washes away naturally. Chase hopes he can continue dodging these propositions so easily. The group inventories Christmas gifts, and trades New Year's Eve war stories. Noah made out with a beautiful girl who pissed the bed later that night.

"And even though she was ripped," Noah says, "she never even let me do anything but stick my tongue down her throat. *That's* top security."

Chase laughs. Noah tells too many stories, interrupts other people's stories, gives too much information and, in general, rambles. But he never makes shit up. If he didn't get anything from the girl, he'll tell you he didn't get anything from the girl, and that she pissed the bed after.

Suddenly they notice a change in the air; the barometer's needle spins. They crane their heads slowly to see Mr. Halliday with his hands on his hips. Making noise in the hall after Check In is forbidden, and they wait to be chastised.

But the floormaster smiles and welcomes them back. "Hey, Chase. Take off your coat and stay awhile."

Chase is unpacking his bags in the room, while Gabriel reads a magazine on the bed. Chase is thinking these guys are his buddies, for real; he felt it the second he saw them. Whatever had begun in that first weird semester has grown into friendship. And they all hold their heads higher; they're no longer novices at Wellington. His unlikely pleasure at being back ratchets up a notch.

As Chase shelves boxers and undershirts washed by his mother, he sees Gabriel's stash of coffee and caramels. Gabriel is still a kid in part; Chase pictures him kneeling on the museum-quality rug in his family's Colombia estate on Christmas morning and plucking ribbons from boxes, grinning.

"So were you dreading coming back?" Gabriel asks now.

It's a tricky question—it would be cooler to dread it than to feel the way Chase feels. "I dunno," he answers. "Not really. Were you?"

Gabriel shrugs. "My sister was driving me crazy so I didn't mind so much."

"Shit, at least I made it back. After finals, which I thought I failed across the board, I was like: *Peace . . . It's been real.*"

"Did you fail any?"

Chase hesitates, ashamed. "I failed geometry, dude. I knew I would. Banks gave me a D-minus for the term, as a favor."

Gabriel hesitates now. "You heard Laine isn't back, right?"

Chase feels a shiver but keeps rummaging in his dopp kit. "Really?" he asks as if this announcement was inconsequential.

"Yeah," Gabriel says. "Guess Wellington caught wind of what went down at 60 Thompson."

Chase never talked about her, even when it would have been natural. Never told anyone what he thought of her. In fact he barely let *himself* in on his own secret. But Gabriel offers up this information diplomatically, with the awareness that he's breaking bad news but the wherewithal not to seem aware.

"Huh. That's too bad," Chase says dully.

Lying in bed, Chase feels rather than sees the dark snow sealing the school. The moon lost behind dirty clouds. Whatever thrill he'd felt is not just gone but turned upside down into bitterness. Now he can't deny why he'd been psyched to come back, because now that it isn't here he feels like shit.

He stares at the ceiling and she stares back. In her big, strange sea-blue eyes is gratitude and confusion and wisdom—which is how she looked at him the night of 60 Thompson. That bad, chemical, immortal night that began with champagne and limousines and glittering snow, and ended with Laine puking on the curb, crying, the green velvet straps of her dress falling off her icy shoulders. When he put her in the cab with Nikki, she'd looked at him—like a little girl and like an ageless soul. On that city street, in that darkest hour buried deeply under the dawn, while wind blew litter through the starry world, Laine Hunt, who needed no one and nothing, looked to him for something.

And so he'd reached for her hand, and held it. When

13

the cabbie looked back with a molten expression to hurry them, he held on still to her hand and then finally let it go. And Laine had smiled at him, and folded into the ripped pleather taxi seat, smiling as they pulled off because he had managed to give her what she'd asked for. It wasn't much and it was everything.

"Goddamnit," he whispers, turning over in his sheets for the hundredth time.

Chase ultimately gets up, stealthily ransacks Gabriel's treasures from break, and opens the window to smoke a cigarillo that makes him woozy within seconds. He doesn't even cup the red coal to keep from being noticed by some insomniac faculty. He flaunts his lawbreaking. He sucks the smoke down so hard ash jumps off the cherry. He lights another off its butt and throws the finished one down, to where it will be found in the morning, a stale brown stub in a melted hole of snow.

He imagines his dad right now, sipping rum and eating pretzels, reading the biography of some secretary of state or ambassador. Sitting in the den where he would catch Chase, usually coming in late, or coming downstairs from his room, stoned, to get vanilla ice cream. His station, where he surveyed the happenings of the family and assumed the worst.

3

The breakfast game of betting on Burns drinking a tall glass of maple syrup, pineapple juice, and ketchup wears off as soon as Chase gets to his first class of the new year. He racks his brain to remember who sweet-talked him into Limnology 101. Of course it was his advisor, Ballast, claiming it would be a great course since the labs took place outside. *And what does that matter if I fail?* Because Mrs. Frederick is waving around diagrams of insects and plankton, and their names, besides being ugly, are elusive, too. He can tell he'll be chasing them down all term on index cards and cheat sheets, because although Chase can think and strategize and synthesize and understand, he cannot memorize.

I will not pass this class.

Chase thinks of his dad, when Chase's sixth-grade

teacher sent a note home about his learning disabilities. His father had scoffed at the letter, saying: "Disabled? Yeah? Is he a quadriplegic? He can't walk or something? My son is not disabled. End of story."

"All right, you guys, you're going to get one partner for the whole semester, and you'll work together for the two-hour Friday labs each week." Mrs. Frederick pushes her bifocals onto her nose and scans her roster. "We're going to do this alphabetically, so when I call your names, go sit with your partner."

Chase Dobbs's eyes slide over to Benjie Durbin. *Oh please, Lord, unite me and Benjie. Granted, he's fifteen and still jokes about farting and bras, and there's cheesecake—look, right there—stuck in his braces as we speak, but I love him. I do. He got every science award there was last term. Benjie Durbin, you are my salvation. I will be nice to you in the hall. Well, I'll acknowledge you, at least. Please God, just this once, throw me a bone.*

"Okay, Mirielle Andonne, you're partners with Abby Benson. Ashley Browning and Randolph Casing. Parker Cole—Parker, is Parker here?"

Everyone mildly scans the room. Frederick taps her list with her pencil, crosses out Parker's name.

"So that puts you, Chase, with Benjie Durbin."

Chase ecstatically gathers his books.

"Do you want me to come over there?" Benjie asks with nasal humility.

"No, no, no," Chase says gregariously. "I'll come to you, Benj. No worries, dude."

And he's halfway across the room when the door opens. And there she is, in a wool mulberry cape, black racing gloves, her cheeks pinked by cold and her flat chest heaving.

"Parker, you're a half hour late almost," Frederick says.

"I'm sorry," she answers, still puffing steam.

"What happened?"

"Craziness," Parker says, shaking her head. "I was making snow angels near Happer Woods and lost my meal card, and I had to dig and dig through the drifts until I found it."

The room snickers quietly.

"But I *did* find it!" Parker says, holding up a wet card.

Frederick seems at a loss. "Well, that's good you found it. Let's see now, this means, Chase, you need to move back to your desk, and Parker, you're going to be his lab partner."

Parker smiles shyly at Chase, who dies a bloody death inside.

Not only will they both fail, he bets, but Parker is a weird girl. They know each other; they've become part of the same loosely joined group of Lower-forms, but out of everyone, he feels most alienated from her. She's smug like a cat, separate, playing the absentminded smart-at-art card too frequently for his taste.

It's not that he doesn't like her. He just doesn't get her. Okay, maybe he doesn't like her a little bit. Parker has *made* herself into an outsider, wearing that mulberry goddamn cape like a bohemian superhero. She acts like she's got one foot in some other world, not hearing her name called because she's doodling French jazz lyrics on her textbook. He once saw her staring ethereally at the half moon in an afternoon sky. *I mean, how much of that can I buy?* Some portion of it had to be performance, the theatrics of persona.

And she stalked, so indignant, past the "popular" tables in the dining hall, never looking their way, sitting as far from them as possible. What did they ever do to her? But if she didn't care or want attention, why the magenta scarf with the ragged rabbit fur jacket, its white tufts dirty with cigarette smoke? Why the top hat she wore one week? If she couldn't see well, why horn-rims when the rest of the world wears contacts?

Sunday morning. The halls of Lancaster are steamy with shampoo, laundry, gossip. Nikki struts in a towel, toothbrush in hand, fresh from the shower.

"Hot damn, gorgeous, what's up?" she asks Parker, who's just stepped from her room.

Parker's wearing the old white coat her aunt Yvonne handed down to her over break. She flashes the red silk lining, which is covered with black letters.

Nikki stops short. "What's that?"

"The lyrics to Hendrix's 'Angel.' You know, the song? I wrote it in Sharpie."

"Why?"

Parker surveys her handiwork with pleasure. She likes that the writing is hidden, and only she'll know it's there. "Why not?" she asks, meaning it. "Hey, what are you doing today? Let's walk to town, you want to? Pancakes are on me. Grandmama slipped a fifty in my Christmas card."

They walk to the village, the fields flanking the road in a raw dazzle. Hands in pockets, steam puffing from their mouths as they laugh. They start off freezing, but actually unbutton the tops of their coats halfway through the walk because of the heat their bodies generate. In the driveway of a home near town, two guys rope snowmobiles into a truck bed, stopping to stare at the girls. Nikki tilts her head back and steps haughtily, and Parker puts her face down, hunches her shoulders—and they both start giggling too soon.

When they're settled on their stools at the diner counter, they rub their hands on their denim thighs to get warm.

"Can I get a tall stack, bacon, and black coffee, please?" Parker asks.

Nikki orders eggs and sausage and OJ, then looks slyly at her friend. "*So,* tell me more about this guy."

"Oh Lord," Parker says, looking away. "Peter?"

"Who else would I mean?"

"I don't know," Parker says, with her usual lack of guile and dexterity in conversation. *It is what it is.*

"Tell me again how he tricked you into kissing him."

The waitress pours coffee into Parker's mug at this moment, and Parker blushes at the woman in the old-fashioned robin's-egg-blue uniform, and hits Nikki too hard on the arm.

"Ow," Nikki says, laughing, cradling her forearm. "It's not a big deal, Park!"

"Sorry," Parker mumbles. She tries to think how to explain Peter. It's funny, no one at Wellington is able to convey "home" very well to anyone else. Stories from "home" are often written in private languages that won't survive translation. Parker can't really explain the topography of her family life this past Christmas. How good her dad, Ben, was, considering it's a time of year when he can get (and has gotten before) depressed, as in: bedridden, sunken-eyed, hopeless. But this year he was his best self, magical and powerful. After listening to Parker rage one afternoon about the dilettantes and snobs and entitled poor little rich kids at Wellington, he'd finally laughed at her. *Park*, he'd said. *You're being a snob as we speak. If a kid's family has money it doesn't necessarily make the kid evil. Come on, sweet pea. Give it a chance.* When her dad is on, he's got the charisma of Santa Claus, Jesus, and Bob Marley combined, and she felt like a spell had been cast on her then.

It was hard to explain what her own town looked like, smelled like, sounded like. Horse shit in the snow by the highway. Church bells clanging between mountains. And she couldn't explain the intricate moments that led up to Peter and Parker in the dank barn on New Year's Eve.

Her parents and his were at Parker's house. Finn, her little brother, was throwing scraps of paper into the big fire in the stone fireplace, and an old scratchy Cream record wobbled around on the turntable, and they drank Ben's home-brewed beer and ate Peter's mom's carrot cake. Somehow, Peter—tall, lanky Peter, bowlegged Peter with the flannel jacket who Parker's known her whole life—somehow Peter, on the pretense of showing her work he'd done on Ben's old Indian motorcycle, got her into her own barn by midnight, got her backed into a dark corner, the rafters mute with bats, got one nervous thigh between hers as they stood in a rookie embrace.

And it's impossible to explain her very first real hookup. "God, it was, I don't know. I can't even describe it."

"How far did you go?" Nikki asks, in her businesslike manner.

"I mean, we got down to underwear. We didn't do everything, you know? But we did what we did for a long time. And I could have done it forever. I could barely walk when we got up, I was, like, *dizzy* from it."

21

"I fooled around with this guy Max at my friend Vanessa's party. And we'd never really been into each other, but we talked forever, we got high, and we just started making out in the kitchen. Nothing big, right? But it was like, that brought us each into existence. Like we didn't exist for each other before that."

"That's exactly it. I've known this guy Peter my whole life, and it's like I didn't know him until that moment."

Parker remembers how infinite the sky seemed, when she and Peter walked out of the barn, opening those big wooden doors to a star-crazy night. The snow burned luminously lavender under the New Year's moon, and the fields scratched and cawed with mysterious, unseen animals.

She's thrown open the doors on a part of life, too, having waited outside for a long time. She always avoided certain conversations in the dorm, never saying she was experienced, but not actually admitting she hadn't done some of the basics.

"I think this semester is going to be different," Nikki says hopefully, running a finger on her plate for a last lick of syrup. "I learned a lot last semester, let's just say that."

"You learned way more than your share. But you know what? Why not get it done early? Now you can move on to the next, because you *get it*."

The waitress puts down their check, and the girls get up, pull gloves and hats from pockets. At the register, they each take a handful of mints.

"Nothing is what it seems to be at this place, right?" Nikki continues. "I mean that in like a good way and bad. I just feel like, I guess it's up to me to make the call. Decide what I want to do at this place, who I'll get to know, who I'll be, all that shit."

"It's crazy, there are a million rules, and yet I feel like I have freedom here. It's a little bizarre," Parker agrees.

Walking back, the sun overhead as ripe as it can get in January, the girls stop in the town park. Parker rolls two cigarettes in numb fingers, and they sit on a stone bench whose cold travels through their flesh. On the iced ground, a Fritos bag is frozen into the dirt like a fossil.

"Did I tell you who my lab partner is?" Parker asks, exhaling.

Nikki shakes her head.

"Chase. And it's so awkward but I don't know why."

Nikki knocks her ash off, thinking. "I like Chase," she says matter-of-factly. "I mean, the kid's running for mayor, it's a little annoying—like, he's got a popularity campaign going that takes all his time and energy. But basically I like him. I think he's decent, a good soul. He just wants people to love him."

"He's got a campaign?" Parker asks in genuine surprise.

Nikki puts her hand over her eyes, shakes her head. "Oh, baby, you kill me."

Parker doesn't understand Chase; she barely knows him. But he's like the sun. Faces tilt to him, whether he speaks or not, to see where he's headed; they're the moons. He throws his iPod on the table, *What's up, y'all*, grinning as if he knows, certainly as if he cares. He throws his feet on the table, latches his hands behind his head, and when a teacher comes by to tell him to put his feet down, he yanks them off the table, gives his doe eyes and a downturned smile.

The only thing that pisses him off, it seems, is when someone plays with his hair. Burns tugged it once, like a schoolboy pulling a girl's pigtail, and Chase went ballistic. He's like a cat, Parker thinks, that likes to be petted, except not in one spot; he'll bite without warning if you touch him there.

He's not her type, this Southern boy, the well-off kid, the prince trying to be a rebel. She fixes him with all kinds of stereotypes about how he probably stereotypes others. She wouldn't like his Republican soul, she thinks. The Confederate flag across his heart. The redneck bumper sticker on his future truck.

When they get back to Lancaster and clomp up the steps in their snowy boots, the floormaster's dog barks and Parker hears Nikki sigh. That dog hasn't yet learned to like Nikki.

She and Laine made up over break, but Nikki didn't

know Laine wasn't coming back till she got here and her stuff was gone. Laine didn't know either until the day before school was starting. Rumors have been whispered in the halls this week about the Crash Test, about the cold roof of that hotel, about Schuyler's guilt or innocence: rumors that are true and rumors that are false and rumors that are both. Rumors that all pivot around Nikki. Parker stands now and watches Nikki throw her NorthFace jacket on the bare mattress that was Laine's bed, run her hands through her long hair. She nods at Parker, expecting her to leave. "See ya, babe."

But Parker goes to her room, gets a faux-fur blanket she's brought from home, and comes back. She holds it up to Nikki. "Let's cover that extra bed, make it a lounging place."

Nikki shrugs. "Sure."

While they're tucking the blanket under the box spring, Nikki says she feels like they're performing some pagan ritual. They laugh a little. But it *is* strange, this empty space. A room alone is what every girl thinks she wants. But the way this happened somehow implicates Nikki, as though she drove away her roommate.

Parker and Nikki lie down on the bed, which is naked no longer. With their faces next to the bristles, they feel like baby animals curled against the mother. They lie there, not talking, just keeping each other Sunday-afternoon company, daydreaming their own private daydreams, strangely natural on the fake mink.

The balls slam the glass walls, and shoes tweak loud and shrill. The banter is muffled inside the greenhouselike boxed courts. Chase is on the JV team with Gabriel, but he can already tell his roommate is much better than he is. This is news. Chase thought he was better than Gabriel at everything, not in a haughty way, just as a matter of fact. Chase is sitting out, leaning back on the blond-wood bleachers, as Gabriel plays Brian from Pakistan. They do the squash waltz, stepping light and fast around each other, to kill the rubber ball against the floor or board.

"Not bad," JD drawls behind him.

"No shit, right? I had no idea," Chase answers the senior.

JD is from San Antonio, a bona fide fairy-tale oil aristocrat's son. His left arm is in a sling like a broken wing, sidelining the three-sport captain for his final year. All the guys secretly try to measure his distress, but JD is an unfathomable character. His face is long and melancholy and wise, unmistakably Texan. His girl, Layla, an old-fashioned beauty with blue-black hair and a rosebud mouth, graduated last year, so he's a widower. This is a phenomenon: the Senior-Year Decline, when a student realizes he got everything good there was to get as an Upper-form and now has shit to look forward to besides moving on.

"I bet you ten dollars he gets moved up to Varsity within weeks," JD says, and he might as well be chewing a stick of hay and pontificating on the chance of rain.

"You think?"

"I do." JD is JV Squash team manager this term, an honorary post and nothing more, the kind given to esteemed but injured athletes. "His strength is there, they just need to keep directing him."

Two members of Girls Squash stroll by, teardrop racquets hanging over their backs, long legs sticking out of white Izod shorts.

"Dang," JD says after they pass.

Chase agrees by nodding his head wistfully. He withholds a grin. *Who the hell says "dang"?* He'd like to say more but is intimidated by JD, as is everyone, including JD's friends. People speak formally to him. People cut him a wide berth. Teachers use a tone of voice with him for some reason that indicates he's a peer.

Chase waits for JD to ask him about Reed, since they knew each other, and since everyone and their mothers like to ask about the older brother. The legend of Reed is like a jack-in-the-box; it springs from ordinary moments (a floormaster's anecdote, one senior girl winking at another as they ask Chase about Reed) with a devil's grin painted on its wooden head. But JD doesn't mention him after all.

"You seeing someone?" JD drawls.

Chase clears his throat, suddenly nervous. "No, not this semester."

"Oh, who were you seeing last semester?" JD asks without malice.

"No, I mean, I wasn't. I wasn't seeing anyone ever. I mean since I got to Wellington."

"Yeah." JD sighs, meaning God knows what. "Winter," he adds, just as enigmatically.

"Yeah, it's pretty cold out," Chase says, thinking: *Wow, this is even worse than talking to a girl. I sound like an absolute moron.* Chase considers mentioning Laine so JD won't think he's a total egg. But before he has a chance, JD switches the subject.

"You're on Two, aren't you?"

"I am."

"Come on up sometime. I'm a proctor on Four. We'll commiserate. If you know what I mean."

"Yeah, definitely," Chase says, having absolutely zero clue, but psyched to be asked up to the JD secret headquarters anyway.

Looking out the Limnology classroom window, Chase sees Parker walking and he feels uneasy. She *makes* him uneasy.

She takes long strides. Measuring the earth, or her passage through it. She's one of those people who doesn't want to take up space but takes up more space than anyone else. She's always squishing down in a chair, which only sends her elbows out and knees up, making her, if anything, more conspicuous.

Like right now. He watches her walking past girls in gray wool coats or cream Patagonia fleeces. Wearing their brown boots from J. Crew, Irish-knit pom-pom hats, argyle mittens. And there's this peacock in a sweeping cape, with a scarlet slash of lipstick, a trail of violet perfume leaving little purple blossoms in her wake like confetti.

Parker's only two minutes late, arriving with snow clumped on her big black boots, steam rolling from her mouth. Chase catches Jonas's eye, a Lower-form and the closest thing to an ally in the room, and they stifle laughter. In that mulberry cape with dead leaves accidentally attached to the hem, fingerless gloves, horn-rim glasses, and a fur trapper's hat, Chase's lab partner looks like an escaped patient from a Moscow mental asylum. She glides past insects pinned to boards, frogs or crawfish or pig fetuses floating in cloudy emulsion, plaster sculptures of the human brain with words scripted on the sections.

"Hi," she says too loudly to Chase as she takes the place next to him, and the class twitters. He barely lifts his hand, acknowledging her but demonstrating reluctance to bond.

Mrs. Frederick holds up beakers for collecting water and picks for breaking ice. She explains their objective today, which is pretty simple. Each team will collect and label samples of water from different lakes, ponds, and rivers. She hands out a list, and Parker and Chase see they've been assigned Dory Lake.

"Make sure you get sediment. That's the good stuff, everybody. The filth. The rich muck. Take a few samples, and mark each tube with exact location of sample-taking. Then compile notes on anything and everything you notice in the vicinity of the sample. Grasses, animals, trees, slopes, drifts, bareness, bald ground . . . Got it?"

If only Parker and Chase knew the experiment they alone would be conducting, an experiment that would have nothing to do with mud, or science. But as the class files out the door, wrapping scarves around their throats and laughing, talking, *no one* could know. As they all walk into the light, which is reflecting off the white snow so brightly that it hurts their faces, and step carefully down broken paths, no one knows anything.

Eventually Parker and Chase are alone, walking under blue firs whose long arms weigh heavily under so much wet white. The quiet is almost loud. Chase kicks at snow.

"Hell, it's cold, don't you think?" he says, shoes soaked and freezing.

Parker smiles, but not at him, relishing the afternoon. "Yeah. I like it."

What a masochist, he thinks. *Or just a Canadian.* And then he thinks with panic: *How on earth are we going to fill these labs with conversation?* He watches her with some jealousy as she steps through gleaming banks like a deer, leaving a concise puncture and nothing else, and lifting her boots out without dragging snow. Chase is thoroughly unpracticed at walking in snowy woods.

"Well, at least you're not making angels and losing your wallet," he says, just to say something.

"Oh, that. I made that up."

He squints at her as she steps in turquoise shade. "You did?" he asks.

"Yeah. I mean, I'd been walking *near* Happer Woods, but I wasn't exactly making snow angels, I was just smoking a cigarette. A bit of truth, though, enhances any cover-up."

Parker had been smoking, and watching squirrels and crows fight for seed. A moment like that is a snow globe to her—contained, isolated, breakable. And her hours and days are strung together like glass beads—dented, handmade, and precious. She's well aware that this makes her separate from the others. It also usually makes her late.

Chase thinks it's funny that she made up a story out of nothing. He never took her for a hustler. "Well, at least you arrived and saved me from Benjie," he says to be polite.

She stops, turns, and looks at him. *Oh, please,* she thinks. *Try harder than that.* Her brown eyes are magnified behind horn-rim glasses. Her cape stops swaying. Parker doesn't say anything, just pulls at her dark hair with one long, pale hand.

And Chase knows that she knows that he lied just now, and then she turns and keeps walking but with less kick in her stride.

He must have looked disappointed when she walked in and Frederick assigned them to be together. All his life, Chase has worn his heart on his face. It got him beaten up by his brother hundreds of times, probably because the trait equaled weakness, and if Reed hated anything, it was weakness. It got him grounded by his dad, over and over, when his excuse didn't match his expression. It got him consoled by his mother, when his bravado didn't come close to concealing his feelings.

Chase picks up a pinecone that's resting on the crust of surface, chucks it with dismal regret and great force, and the featherweight thing lands two feet away. Maybe he should just come clean.

"Park, it's not that I didn't want to be your lab partner. It's just that I'm totally going to fail this course. It's that simple, you know what I mean? I was praying to *God* Benjie would save my ass."

"Why are you going to fail?" she asks without turning to face him.

"I have zero capacity for memorization. I mean, just no way to remember."

Now she spins around, cape twirling. "There're always

ways to remember, Chase."

His turn to look at the ground. He kicks at fluffy snow. She's a funny bird. Suddenly, out of nowhere, he gets slammed into the snow. He flounders, laughing, wiping snowflakes from his mouth, unable even to protest, too surprised.

She stands, laughing, pointing. "That's what you get, Dobbs!" she says. "For not wanting to be my partner. Now we're even."

"Is that right?" he asks innocently from his sitting position.

She nods her head earnestly. And before she can protect herself, she is tackled to the white ground, shrieking about her glasses and the beakers, laughing hysterically.

Catching their breaths, sprawled on the field, they stare at the lake, now visible on the near horizon. It's so loaded with snow that as a body of water it's only recognizable by its ring of iced grasses and brambles, and the indent where the lake meets its borders.

"You ready to collect some 'rich muck,' young lady?" Chase drawls, as they brush themselves off and limp to the destination. Chase pushes his streaked brown hair behind his ears and pulls the Bass fishing hat from his inside coat pocket. The bill is bent sharply down the middle and makes his face narrower and more symmetrical.

"Thrilled," she answers. "I've been waiting my whole life for this. It's sure to be a scientific breakthrough."

Later, when they analyze this next moment, or when they dream of it, or when they lie in bed and can't sleep and can't dream *because* of it, both of them will have trouble remembering who saw what first. How they knew what they suddenly knew. Because all it looked like at first blink was a shiny rod sticking out from center ice.

"What is that?" Parker says quietly, and neither of them is steady on their feet all of a sudden.

"Not sure," Chase says, moving automatically closer even though he'd rather turn and run.

The shaft standing out of the ice has a curved tip. It looks like, it almost looks like–

"It looks like a *ski*," Parker says doubtfully, glancing at Chase.

He starts to move fast, rushing to the bank, testing the ice beyond the grass. It squeaks, groans. It splits under his weight, and he pulls back his foot. Parker comes running too, shades her eyes to better see what the ski is attached to. There–a bit of green, a hue nature doesn't make, not in the dead of winter at least. A jacket.

Parker suddenly realizes that Chase is trying again to go out there. "Stop! Chase, *no*, you can't do that."

He keeps going.

"Chase!" Now Parker sounds hysterical enough to get him to turn.

"What?" he asks.

She looks at him. "You can't walk on that ice."

He looks around then at the hills, the woods, the empty landscape. He calls for help, in a voice that is raw, crude, and new.

Parker starts to run back to the school. "I'll go, you stay. Chase do *not* go on the ice," she calls over her shoulder. "That would not be brave, that would be stupid," she says desperately. Then she stops still to ask him: "Promise me."

"*What?*"

"Chase!" she shouts, angry now. "Promise not to walk on the ice."

"I promise."

He stands at the shore. He looks helplessly from the shining stake to the mulberry cape that decreases in size. The sky is so wide and hungry he resists putting his arms across his face to prevent the world from seeing him, the way a child believes pulling a sheet over his head makes him invisible. Instead, Chase waits. Caught in a purgatory between Brave and Stupid—a place many a man before him has gotten lost.

Mary Loverwest. Redhead. Upper-form.

She actually liked taking Latin. *Amo Amas Amat.* A teacher had once explained that studying the system of a language, even if the language is dead, expands the mind's capacity for understanding other systems. For thinking. For knowing.

On her bed a teddy bear, suckled and rubbed down to

silk, its stuffing visible through the skin. Mary wore vanilla body lotion. She brushed her fire-red hair with a sterling silver heirloom comb handed down by her father's mother, and monogrammed with Jemimah Loverwest's initials. Mary came from Minnesota. She'd kissed three guys in her life, and allowed one—as they tumbled one hot afternoon in Happer Woods—to put his hands up her skirt, fumble over the underwear's waistband, and reach inside as though looking for something that he lost. Meanwhile she'd stared at the pinpoints of sky that burned through the tree canopy, almost smiling, feeling rather divorced from the goings-on, from his hands, from love itself.

And that would be it. That afternoon. Instead of long years of turbulent teenage relationships, breakups and make-ups through college and on into adulthood in some big jungle of a city, years of courtship culminating in a long marriage, the dawning of sexual and emotional wisdom, the fruition of love and devotion—instead of all that, Mary Loverwest got one afternoon, got a boy searching between her thighs with more agitation than lust, got a bemused study of the sky from a strange position.

Neither Parker nor Chase knew her. Once, Parker stood behind her on line in the dining hall, watched her bite into an apple that was rotten and make a face, then laugh as she held up the fruit to her friend. *Gross! Look what I just ate!*

Ironically, she was a record-setting swimmer, with big,

round shoulders and rock-hard calves. The butterfly was her favorite stroke, and she undulated through misty, chlorine pools as if she was born to do it. No, neither Parker nor Chase have ever seen Mary swim. They have only seen her drowned.

4

The Loverwest family is delayed getting to Wellington by another dump of snow. The memorial service is held in the church, sun streaming through purple windows onto downturned heads, as friends and teachers speak about Mary. The father stares at each speaker as if they might answer the riddle tormenting him, and on each side of his mouth is a deep line carved into skin, like the ones on a ventriloquist dummy's wooden face. Chase wonders if Mr. Loverwest always had those lines—or if they just happened and now would be there forever.

Chase sees Parker standing with Nikki. Parker's wearing some old black silk thing that looks like the suit of a Victorian librarian. She seems distraught, guilty, as though she'd planned the disaster.

Someone in the choir loft, unseen, sings a Cat Stevens song in a strong and unisex voice, unaccompanied by instruments, as people exit. *Oh very young, what will you leave us this time. You're only dancing on this earth for a short while . . .*

Outside, everyone shuffles in dirty snow, in dark clothes. Some carry flowers, red blossoms curling up against the cold.

Chase wants to feel sad. Good old-fashioned sorrow, that's what he believes he should experience. But instead he's angry and skittish, unable to meet people's eyes. He hates how he's turned overnight into some kind of celebrity, for having found her. He hates seeing Mary's shining cross-country ski every time he's about to fall asleep. He hates watching Susanna Marks bask in bizarre attention for having been the deceased's best friend. There are unknown adults lurking about the grounds, lawyers and PR people and board members, congregating in back rooms to handle the tragedy, to shape the way the incident will play out at school and in the newspapers. Their presence agitates Chase.

To Parker, Mary's like a black hole that moves about campus, a shade that passes through marble halls, that slips across the lit auditorium stage, that takes up space in the white-tiled showers. Everything falls into the hole; it absorbs life from the rest of them.

It's a shadow, sucking up ordinary things—a piece of toast with grape jelly, a new manga, a Shetland sweater. All the miracles it can't have anymore.

Parker and Nikki lie on the fur bed, eating stale birthday cake that had been left in the hall after a feed. They get icing crumbs all over the blanket, as they try to put pieces in their mouths while lying down. They talk about fate for over an hour, but strenuously avoid mentioning Mary or death.

When Dean Mariah Braden approaches him about undergoing grief counseling, Chase thanks her and explains that he doesn't need it. Dean Braden clears her throat, her hands in the pockets of a red tweed coat, but doesn't look away from his eyes.

"Chase, you actually are required to have five sessions."

He looks around in disbelief. They're standing in the windowed hall, and outside a snowplow shovels wet clumps. "Required by who?"

"The school."

The school. Who's that? It's a composite of dead guys who wrote Wellington's rule book, their ancestors who brought the value system in a trunk on the ship from England, hotshot lawyers, the phantom parents of the student body, the hypothetical parent who sues the institution because his child gets depressed after an "incident" such as discovering a drowning victim, and it's the pages of psychological reports handed out at the last crisis-management-in-American-schools meeting. *That's* who demands he go sit in a room with a therapist and explain Mary's ski, shining in the winter light, and explain how a shining ski represents everything, how it has become the emblem of everything delicate and dangerous that passes through his heart these cold days.

"Okay?" Braden prompts, with protocol compassion.

Chase is about to say *Well, yeah, it's okay since I don't have the choice of it being not okay.* "I mean . . . ," he begins, trails off.

"What's your objection? Let me ask you that."

"I just don't feel like I'm being asked to come in because anyone worries about me or thinks I'm upset or cares about Mary or whatever. It's because the school cares about its own name and stuff, and wants to do damage control."

"Why do you think that?"

"Well, for example, it's not like anyone from the school talked to me personally, and thought I should see a therapist. It's just being done according to procedure and stuff."

"We *are* talking personally right now, don't you think?"

Chase is about to say that this is anything but a personal conversation, but he knows this will trigger more concern that he's a liability.

So he makes a sad mouth. He banks on the effect of his slow-burn smile, lets his lips curl, feels his eyes sparkle darkly. "Of course," he relents, *knowing what's good for him.*

Braden is barely convinced by his charming pain.

Luke Gregson: "Hey, Chase, you should be on *Law & Order* or some shit."

Tibbet Thulin: "Bet her high beams were on, right, Chase?"

Jennifer Hyland: "I know you did it."

A week passes and the jokes come out. They blossom out of silence. It's the Tourette's of any community repressed by the etiquette of mourning. But Chase doesn't want to laugh yet, and occasionally gives a venomous look, but says nothing.

The kids cracking comments remind him of himself and his buddies when they were young: throwing rocks at a bees' nest in a peach tree, the nest quivering in the sweet, hot shade, the boys wanting to wake the sticky hive, wanting to make something happen, and fearing it. Throw a rock, duck, look.

Run.

His first counseling session takes place Tuesday evening, in a room behind the infirmary. The sun crackles ruby red on the wintry horizon, the trees black scratches on the sunset.

He slumps in a chair, long legs stretched out and crossed at the shin, eyes narrowed imperceptibly.

The therapist asks him to call her Karen.

"Hi, Karen," he says dutifully, scrubbing his tone clean of any sarcasm.

"Do you know why we're here?" she purrs.

"I imagine we're here so that the Wellington School is protected from a lawsuit my parents could bring if I get depressed, or something like that."

"Is that what you think?" Karen rubs her braid with one thumb.

"I think we're here to talk about Mary."

After a pause Karen asks: "What would you like to say about Mary?"

"I'd like to say that I respect her memory and don't want to talk about her."

And that's the most productive part of their hour. The rest is spent in uncomfortable silences as Chase looks away from her questions. The sun dies, and he can't see out the window; the landscape succumbs to his stark reflection.

But at the end he decides to get a return on his time, and he asks Karen when Mary is thought to have died.

"Her roommate said she left before her first class to do a cross-country ski workout. She probably fell through the ice around seven thirty, they think."

Chase likes Karen's no-frills answer.

"Did she die, I mean literally, from hypothermia?" he continues.

"She most likely died from inhaling the icy water. Her body was shocked by the cold into gasping for air, and instead she got water. That's usually the cause of cold-water drowning."

"I see," Chase muses, getting a grip on this visual. He's been fixating on the mechanics, the exact details of how Mary died, and if they could have done anything.

When he leaves the room, Parker's waiting in the foyer. She's wearing Adidas sweatpants under a canary-yellow vintage coat, the sweats crumpled above the rims of black boots, and on her head is a white scuffed fedora with a pheasant's feather. Absentmindedly she carves gibberish with a ballpoint pen into the wooden arm of the chair. He slips by.

When he arrives for his second session the next week, he can hear voices, and moves closer, slumps in the chair next to the door. Parker's in there. It takes a minute to pick apart the sounds and distinguish words.

"Are we done yet?" Parker asks.

"Five more minutes."

"I'm sorry."

"It's okay, I didn't get you in here to force you to talk."
Silence.

"I guess I have one question," Parker says, and then

poses something to Karen that Chase can't hear.

"How do you mean?" Karen asks after a moment.

"Like, is it possible, you know, that she was *trying* to do it."

"To drown herself?"

"Yeah."

"I don't think so. It's statistically not a method people use, and I personally don't get that sense, but it's an understandable question, Parker."

"But isn't there some chance that she knew she was, like, pushing boundaries, or tempting fate? Might she have been, like, half determined?"

Hmm, Chase thinks. *I'm obsessed with the How and the When. Parker wants to know the Why.*

When she comes out, Parker's back is turned to Chase. Karen's holding a date book, scanning a page with a pencil's tip.

"That was great, Parker. We have three more sessions, and then you can decide whether you want to continue. Does next week same time work?"

Parker puts her long hands in the pockets of the yellow coat. "I'm actually done, I think, but thanks."

Karen blinks at the girl. "No, I meant, you have to have three more sessions."

Parker doesn't move. "I don't want to come to any more sessions, so you can have someone send a letter home or whatever but from here I'll deal with this myself."

Karen watches, stupefied, as Parker turns away.

Chase recognizes on Parker's face the same dry-eyed vibe he feels. They exchange some strange communication without words, and it fortifies Chase to stand up and tell Karen that he's done too.

"Come on, now, Chase. This isn't monkey see, monkey do," Karen chides.

"I never wanted to come in the first place."

He hurries to catch up with Parker, who's startled to see him tagging along. "Did you just, are you not going to that session?" she asks with a slow smile.

He shakes his head. They high-five.

"Hungry?" he asks.

"Yeah," she says.

They hit the snack bar, which is scarcely populated. They get microwaved popcorn and root beer, and sit at a table looking out the window onto the windy twilight.

"It's not that *she* was bad," Parker says. "I just didn't want to be forced to talk about it *that way*. I felt like the school was trying to control my emotions, even though that sounds a little crazy."

"No, she wasn't bad. I bet she gets kids in there all the time who don't want to be there. It's not like we're the first."

Their conversation is erratic, but they're both comfortable with silences. As if what they discovered on the lake has catapulted them past small talk and bullshit. Parker brushes crumbs off her cheek, looks at her watch. "Study hall's in ten minutes."

Chase stretches as he stands, yawns. "Okay, kid. See you around."

"Yeah, see you around," she says, as she gets her things together and watches him walk away. Broad shoulders. Heels scuffing. Long hair. *Why on earth am I shivering?*

Chase has never seen a girl fully naked in person, from close enough to understand what that means. But he mentally owns an accidental pastiche of daydreams, bits of visions he's caught in dark rooms while making out, pieces of films and porn magazines and other guys' stories. These images sometimes roll unheralded through his mind like a slide show. The pictures click by so fast he can't ever get a look, but he still viscerally perceives the bodies, the limbs, the rosebud mouths, tufts of hair between thighs, lace, straps, an eye. A hand–reaching for him or pulling him down, or pushing him away. It's a scatter of possibility, a wishy-washy promise of pleasure, a bill of lading for goods that might never be delivered.

Recently Laine has featured prominently. Not as a whole, but as a ghost of parts flitting through the shots. White-blond hair pulled back in a ribbon. Muddy legs pumping under a field hockey skirt on the field. The sun-blanched hair on her golden arm.

But at some point, a slide of Mary's body—as he somehow conceives of it, recovered but not living—gets slipped into the revue. He jolts upright whenever this is shown—whether he's in bed, or in class, or slouching on bleachers waiting his turn on court. Against an ivory backdrop of snow, a redhead is drawn from a dark pit, and she's not wearing skis or a green jacket or anything—but a sheen of ice. Her body blue with cold, kelp wrapped like anklets of emerald fur around legs, lips pale and plump, eyes somehow crying still.

One dark afternoon, he sits in the fourth-floor common room, the one no one goes to as it's televisionless and its ceiling slopes attic-style. He tries to force this unwanted picture out of his head, because he's scaring himself each time it arrives. He tries to evict it from his brain with sheer muscle, and it feels like bending iron bars with bare hands.

Noah has appeared on the threshold, his tall form bent. "Hey, Anne Frank," he says, running his hands through his stiff black hair. "Let's hit it. What the fuck are you doing up here? It's taco night."

Chase looks in the musky light at his friend. "Screw off, you piece of shit."

Noah freezes, having never heard Chase like this. Last semester, Chase convinced most of Cadwallader 2 to get a

Red Card to watch the *Godfather* trilogy together. And Chase always took the left glove, since they only had one pair, during the boxing matches in the showers. When someone feels shitty, they hit Chase's room for a chew, and Chase cracks joke after joke until the misery is dissipated— like it's his *job*. When Russell Jenkins found out his parents were moving the family to Japan, Russell included, Chase took him to dinner in town, brought him back relaxed and happy.

But maybe Chase just needed to spit some venom, because he feels instantly better. He cracks his best smile. "I'm kidding, bro. I'm *starved*."

Noah's quiet as they walk the hall. "I know you've had a rough go. If you need anything, just say it."

"Thanks, man. It's weird. It's not like I knew the girl. I don't know why I'm affected by it."

"You want to just hang in the dorm and I'll grab you food?"

"Naw, I'm really fine, just hungry."

They clatter down the stone steps and break into the dusk, run to the dining hall, and Chase is suddenly exhilarated to be exhilarated by a prospect as simple as chili con carne.

The next morning, Chase sees Burns outside his window, building a snowman. *How strange,* Chase thinks, *almost innocent.* And then Burns puts on the finishing touch: a carrot stick jutting out from between the ice sculpture's loins. This sends him from the decent mood he'd somehow regained into a midway state. A fuzzy misanthropic icky feeling.

That night, Chase remembers something his mom said over Christmas break. He'd come home from early-morning fishing with his dad, the truck spewing gravel as they braked in the drive. The windows were mostly obscured by hedges, azaleas and rhododendrons, their leaves sequined with cool dew. Both he and his dad knew she was inside because in some intangible way, the house looked completely different when she wasn't home. Depleted, or dangerously empty. She was the heart of that world.

"Hey, Ma," Chase said, as he came into the room.

"Sweetheart," she said, and gave him a long appraising look.

Vivien was sitting in the den under her reading light, eating raspberries from an English china dish, reading the antique cloth-bound Hemingway book in her lap. Her chicory coffee's fragrance filled the early rooms.

She coaxed him close so she could push his hair back behind his ears, and kept looking at his face, obviously concentrating on a memory. "Chase, honey, do you remember the silver ring I used to set in the icebox, and you teethed on it?"

He blushed, for no reason.

"Oh, you're going to have quite a year, sugar. Your teeth are surely coming in right now."

Chase knocks on JD's door Sunday afternoon. He feels weird, like he's calling on a girl. JD answers, welcomes him into a dorm room that somehow has the aura of a somber parlor complete with mahogany gun cabinet and humidor and brass liquor cart, although in reality JD has none of these things.

JD is making *café de olla*, he explains to Chase. It's coffee simmered for hours in the pot, with cloves and cinnamon. He pours two mugs, dexterously considering the sling, and they sit in leather chairs in the half dark. Late-day sunshine pools like marmalade in valleys of white. The buildings in shade are caked in pale blue crumbs of snow. When Chase takes a sip, he almost chokes.

"It's strong," JD says, his hangdog eyes half lidded as he takes his own sip but looks at Chase.

"Dude. This and a joint, you're good to go."

But JD looks severely at him. "I don't smoke. I'm not into drugs really," he adds.

"No, me neither," Chase lies.

"My dad has Mexican coffee every morning," JD says.

"It's perfect," Chase says. "Your dad is onto something."

"Oh, my dad's onto a lot of things," JD says with that moody snicker. "It's wild; he comes from less than nothing.

God dang, he was born in an artichoke field. My grand-parents were migrant workers."

"Are you serious?" Chase asks, nursing his hot drink. Most people hide their past, if that past isn't glamorous, and it's interesting to hear someone brag about adversity.

"His three siblings, they all died as kids. He's the only one who made it. And he definitely made it."

Chase politely asks if JD and his father are close.

"We are," JD says in his solemn way. "I'm not as good a man as he is, because I haven't gone through what he went through."

JD is a certain kind of Texan, who can wear cologne and carry Hermès luggage and say profound things that are one degree away from Hallmark cards, and it all enhances his masculinity. Often, between statements, he semiscowls, as if trying to work something out, an equation so long it dou-ble-loops in his head, crosses over itself, gets knotted.

"I sit here," JD says, "and I know we're lucky, man. You know? We definitely have to make good on this opportu-nity."

Chase decides those sound like words JD's heard often. Although he waits for him to continue on this thread, that's the end. Instead JD jokes about History 209 last year, when Mrs. Vincent was taking melatonin as a sleep aid, except she fell asleep whenever she darkened the room for slide shows, lying with her head on the desk and her legs splayed as she snored like a dog. JD knows how to enter-tain; he's like a junior Frank Sinatra, mannered and coarse at the same time. His storytelling fills the room, and Chase is grateful, sensing that JD means to take his mind off things.

After a while the two of them sink into stillness, and just listen to David Grisman's mandolin pluck its way over folk songs, carve notes like smoke in the twilight, draw a faraway tale of mountains, hills, trees, moons, plains. Chase is sud-denly rejuvenated, in an unusual and simple way. He sits and feels redder blood running through his veins.

5

Parker loves art lectures. The lights-off hush in the room, the teacher's clear voice stealing over silhouettes at desks with their chins resting on their folded arms. The tap of the stick. The whir and click of slides. The blossom of an artwork onto the screen, the beam telescoping from the lens.

A guy arrives late, hurries to his seat, and while walking down the aisle, an Edward Hopper painting is cast onto his back. The lonely door, the empty street, the red porch. He sits, and the house is properly cast on the roll-down screen again.

"There is a sense in Hopper's work, the works, that is, which aren't peopled, that someone is waiting somewhere offstage. Inside the train station. Behind the curtain. In the back of the car. You look at this door, here. Just a tablet of darkness. Who's in that house?"

The class stirs to answer, voices coming from unseen faces. But Parker suddenly and very simply realizes who's in the house.

Mary. And she knows that from now on, Mary will be in all the houses, in all the hiding spaces, in all the deep and unknowable places in life, in art, in dreams. That's where Mary has now moved. And this doesn't upset Parker but rather consoles her. She's glad the girl has a home.

The projector's light picks up strands of Parker's hair, sets them on electric fire.

Valentine's Day is on the horizon. A red heart of sun peeking over the snow, sending crimson fingers into pale rooms.

The ancient hush of books hides a warren of sleek, techno-glam rooms compactly built into the old ribs of the pine and marble library. Leather chairs, whose arms are studded with iron buttons, are blanched by winter light falling through arched windows.

Wellington is more a military school by philosophical design than a typical high school, except regarding students' schedules, when it's closer to a liberal arts college. Wellington students choose their classes; some seniors become so skilled at this that they manage to schedule classless Fridays. For those less experienced, the rule of thumb is to clump free periods for a *sense* of freedom.

Free periods are good for sleeping, cramming for the next class, nicotine fixing, or releasing sexual tension, but for Chase, the space between geometry and English is for fantasy basketball league, and he uses the computers in the library to play. Since Burns set up the league with a buy-in of 150 bucks, Cadwallader has been following the NBA as closely as their I-banking parents follow the Dow. Right now, Chase is deciding whether to start Elton Brand or Antawn Jamison when he notices a message in his inbox.

> *From: Laine Hunt*
> *To: Chase Dobbs*
> *Subject: Francais*
>
> *Hey Chase.*
>
> *I haven't had the chance to say sorry about what happened after the Gold and Silver. I hope I didn't ruin everyone's night. As you probably heard, Dean Talliworth thought it might be "in my best interest" to take a little time off. But, he also said if I kept up with work and did OK on the midterms, I may be able to come back in the spring. So, we'll see.*
>
> *He gave me my class lists and I noticed we're in Mr. Monteleone's French 201 together. I'm responsible for getting the homework assignments. I guess it's*

his little way of trying to punish me. I hate to ask this,
but will you e-mail me the assignments? Please let me
know.

    Thanks,
    Laine

Even though he's surprised, in some way, deep down, he'd known this would happen. He'd been waiting for it. And the pleasure of this development runs through him like melted silver.

He has a strange memory suddenly, unbidden, of his grandfather offering him as a kid a sip of a cocktail. They were on a porch of a river house, in that golden space between afternoon and evening. The drink was palest blue; it was crème de menthe and vodka, and it was awful. But the aftereffect was nice: a creamy, cold forgetting. He could feel the liquid burn through him, straight to his heart. It almost hurt.

The idea of Laine, the blond hair and blue eyes and small, wet mouth, her strength, even her banishment—it's all intoxicating. Chase types slowly, choosing his words. French may have just become his favorite class.

From: Chase Dobbs
To: Laine Hunt
Subject: RE: Francais

Salut Laine,

No worries. Everyone was super buzzed that night. Noah passed out in his tux and his maid undressed him, and Gabe ended up pissing in the Michonne's hallway closet on some famous artwork. The retard thought it was the bathroom. I'm just amazed we somehow made it back to the apt. Anyways, I'd be happy to e-mail you the assignments. Pas de problem. Monsieur Monteleone is a croaky old bitch, so I'm not surprised he's making things difficult. Let me know if you need anything else from the inside. Enjoy your freedom!

Later,

C

Chase busts outside, late to English since he took a lot of time perfecting his e-mail to Laine. Hands in his pockets, he might as well be whistling a happy tune; Chase is in his modern-Tom-Sawyer mode, king of possibilities.

Granted his mood can swing fast, like a samurai sword, and with no warning. He can fall into the "indigo state," blues so dark they're deeper than blue. That's when he wants to lock himself in a basement and light every match in a matchbook, one by one, then blow them out. Listen to Kings of Leon at ear-bleeding volume. Focus his hatred like a laser beam: at his father, the school, some senior asshole who messed with him in the dining hall. That's when he stays in his room, picks blackheads in the mirror till his skin bleeds. When he's in that mode, he's sure not to think of girls at all, in case the mirror he's gazing in is glass on the other side (like in a police investigator's room), and the girl can see the ugly Chase.

Chase sees JD heading to Cadwallader across Senior Grass, a plot located between the main building and the dorms, and reserved for seniors to walk on. The idea of bunkering in JD's room, with its older-student aura and exclusivity, is enticing. A way to maintain the good mood.

"C, what's up? Where you off to?" JD calls to him.

"Nothing. Got out of class with Ballast so I have a free period," he lies, in hope of an invite to go chew in the dorm or something.

"Come on." JD waves Chase onto the mound, which is tufted with crusty, icy blades. "Cross with me."

Chase pauses, remembering Noah's recently regrown eyebrow, payback for a solo cross from puck-head seniors. "You sure?"

"Yeah, man. Get your skinny ass up here."

Chase reluctantly hops on the shortcut.

JD gives Chase a smile. "What do you say we go have a dip instead?"

Chase weighs his options. *Well, it's only my first cut. I'll need four more before detention and a letter home,* he justifies. "Sounds like a plan."

"Thattaboy." JD pats his back with a rancher's glove as they head toward the dorms. "You got a fresh can?"

"Nah. Sorry." Chase is pretty sure he's heard JD ask this before.

"It'd be a lot cooler if you did." JD winks and Chase laughs, acknowledging the *Dazed and Confused* quote. "That's okay. Let's go to my room. I think I know where we can find some Bear."

Chase's dad steps forward in his head like a hologram to lecture him: *I wish I could say it was your choice, son, to fail or succeed this year, because that's what a lot of fathers would open up with. But you know what, Chase? It's not your goddamn choice. End of story. It's my money paying that tuition bill, and it's my choice how you'll perform.*

Ditching class to have a midday lipper with a senior probably isn't the performance he expected.

But Chase also has the out-of-body experience that Laine can see him walking with JD. He sees a movie of himself walking stoically in the cold with the senior. Then he catches himself doing this and feels semi-ashamed. He does this a lot, picturing Laine picturing him. *Christ, I thought I said good-bye to imaginary friends years ago.*

The two guys kick it in JD's room, sucking on dank tobacco, joking about a girl whose skirt had been tucked into the waistband of her tights when she walked into chapel that morning.

"Oh, dang. That shit is funny." JD sighs after they collect themselves.

The daylight burns gold through heavy shades, and Chase feels wiser and worldlier by his proximity to the Cadwallader cowboy.

Burns sees him leaving JD's room though, and asks if it was good for both of them.

"Blow me," Chase mutters.

He does make it to limnology class that Wednesday. The class is still tainted, like a red scrim was pulled down and the class darkened by Mary. Chase and Parker definitely wear the crowns of king and queen of that tragedy. The class sits with their books open and discusses the stages of naiads.

As they walk out after the bell rings, Chase comes over to Parker in solidarity.

"How's my buddy Parks today?" he says, slinging his arm over her shoulders. "Gearing up for V-Day?"

She smiles but otherwise freezes, suddenly smelling the wool of his coat, the amber whiff of nicotine on the cuffs, the essence of winter embedded in the fibers, and feeling his arm burn through his clothes and through her clothes to her own arm.

Nikki hates being alone, and often tracks Parker down to the art studio where she works on her Independent Study. The raccoon coat is piled carelessly in the corner. Nikki has a coffee for each of them, and they pry off the lids, blow steam from the top.

"Thanks, baby," Parker says, trying a hot sip. "Ouch."

Nikki's staring out the huge window at dull whiteness. The hedges and the vegetable garden are clotted with wet snow. The world is in deep hibernation, showing no signs of life. "Goddamn. This country living is killing me, Park."

"I know. I ate chocolate cake for lunch, and that's a sign that things aren't quite working for me."

"You know, Chase was flirting big-time with you at lunch, by the way," Nikki says, turning to face Parker.

Parker gives her a look that makes Nikki apologize. "It's a compliment, girl, *Jesus*," Nikki defends herself.

Parker stares a second, the wet brush in one hand. Then she smiles. "Was he?"

"Um, yeah, can't you tell?"

Parker goes back to painting, a grin on her face. But then she turns to Nikki, worried all over again. "Do *not* get involved, Nik. Please. No matchmaking stuff that you're so good at."

"I would never!"

"You would."

Nikki sips her coffee, gives Parker puppy dog eyes. Parker points her brush at her friend, tries to make a menacing face. "Promise me."

"I promise," Nikki says too quickly. Then adds more seriously: "I promise."

Doors bang down the hall. Nikki moves around Parker's easel to see what she's doing. There's a stark outline of a male figure in black paint, and an unmarred white background. But inside the lines is Parker's replication of a Monet; a field of purple irises is crammed into the body.

"Do you like it?" Parker asks.

"I do," Nikki says, although her voice isn't confident. "I don't know if I *get* it, but I like it."

"It's, like, if someone loves a place, or has lived somewhere, that all becomes a part of him. That's what I imagine, or something like that."

"Hmm," Nikki says. "Glad you're in charge here, not me. I don't know how you think this shit up, girl."

Parker likes that Nikki sticks around for the next half hour. They make some conversation, and are silent part of the time. They walk back through the early dusk, their voices loud under the sky, which hangs low and close, like a canopy. That's winter in New England. A sky so heavy with itself it's threatening. Birds have trouble breaking into it.

* * *

Chase walks through the music wing to the mail room; barely audible instruments from different rooms make an eerie song. It's strange to be down here during daylight, as it's a notorious nighttime zone. The music wing, with its private practice rooms, is a no-tell motel. Keys have been bought, borrowed, copied, and passed down for decades. The aura of sexual wrongdoing is thick.

Chase isn't expecting mail, just maybe another fax from his father to call home. His father "doesn't do e-mail" but the frequency of his secretary's faxes has increased recently. Mr. Ballast, Chase's faculty advisor and his teacher, *double whammy*, had called Mr. Dobbs after Chase's first absence from class. Chase feels betrayed by his advisor. Ballast had been the one adult who spoke to him like a friend.

On the announcement board near the mailboxes are upcoming games, babysitting gigs for faculty kids, and tutoring sessions. A letter in the "free speech" case has been posted by Elizabeth Davis, an Upper-form. She pleads with the student body to remember Mary Loverwest, and not let the girl get sucked down into PR damage control and articles on the school. The letter writer reminisces about Mary in a disingenuous way. *I wish people would get their grubby hands off her,* Chase thinks, and it's not the first time—there's been a barrage of ideas and memories foisted on her. He turns away in disgust.

It reminds him of a marble statue in a Charleston fountain, a white stone body with white eyes. Once, someone spray-painted obscenities on her belly. Occasionally someone painted her toenails red with polish. Especially because Chase had grown up with her, it seemed so wrong. This luxurious woman, standing vulnerable and alone inside snow drifts of pale pink azaleas, should be untouchable.

When he opens his mailbox, he finds a red rose.

"I don't know, I just might have the urge to go, I can't tell yet," Parker says to Nikki.

They're standing in Parker's room, where Parker is trying on a pile of dresses Nikki brought over. Outside the snow falls in wet clumps from the electric blue sky. Parker is being coy, as she betrayed too much the other day in the art studio about Chase. She doesn't want anyone to know she has feelings for him. He's a cliché, straight out of a boarding-school brochure. *Why do I care?*

"Do you want to go with someone?" Nikki fishes.

"Not necessarily. Do you?" Parker desperately turns it around.

"Hell, I don't know. I kind of want to get dressed up and stuff, but there's no one I want to go with." Seth sent her white roses this morning but this is something that Nikki isn't willing to talk about.

"I hear you," Parker says, although that's not how she feels at all. Not only does she want Chase to ask her, she has a sixth sense that he will.

Trying on the dresses is a weirdly intimate experience. Parker can smell beer and anxiety on them, can feel the days and nights through which they were worn. The dresses are like diary entries. Pin-the-tail-on-the-donkey at a boring birthday party in a ranch house that smelled like dog. Spilled Southern Comfort in a limousine to a Metallica show. A sweet sixteen party that ended at Denny's at five A.M., and with a ketchup stain. A bar mitzvah in the heat of summer.

A bead is missing here, a sequin gone from there. At the top of the zipper the metal clasp is broken—from a guy in a hurry, or a girl in a rush to get in pajamas and slam off the lights before her dad makes it up the stairs, or climbing in a kitchen window after being out all night.

Nikki throws them at Parker, begs her to wear them. It's so Nikki: *Here, take my dresses, take my confidence, take my experience . . .*

The main problem is bust size. The tops hang a bit, like husks. Parker holds them up and looks at Nikki with sad eyes. "I want to wear one, Nik, I do."

"You have to! They look great."

"Come on, Nik. There's, like, a tumbleweed blowing around the tops."

Parker pulls on the last dress, a midnight-blue H&M halter. When she adjusts the strings that tie around her neck, the dress looks divine. Nikki cases it up and down. "That's the one."

So Parker pulls off her Adidas sneakers with the gold tongue. She'd been wearing them as a safety blanket as she got undressed in front of her friend. She needs now to match heels with the dress. Parker has a collection of vintage heels that reflects a catalog in her mind of archetypal ladies: Hitchcock heroine, or seventies secretary, or Bryn Mawr student in the late sixties. Aquamarine pumps someone could have worn in a Kansas motel murder. Rhinestone sandals for dancing across a Morocco square. Violet ballet flats to wear while smoking joints and painting in your attic studio.

She rummages through the closet. Finally she puts on a pair of dark pink vintage ankle strap stilettos, and they both stare at the transformed girl in the mirror. *This is it.*

Bitter cold day, wind practically tearing stone molding off buildings. Burns is ruling their table. His left hand is covered in eczema. Chase rolls his eyes to himself, so sick of him. He gets worse every day, bossier, louder, as if *he* was the one who founded this group.

Mirielle, who grew up with Burns in Rye, told Chase that Burns was a cartoon rich kid. A Jamaican man drove him to elementary school in a Silver Cloud, Mummy and Daddy brought him to the family box seats at every opera and ballet in New York, there were bells on side tables and silver domes on dinner plates, and a servants' quarters behind the tennis courts. The family is like a set of moths pinned to velvet, formaldehyde-soaked specimens of a social class that barely exists anymore in a world of CEOs in Levi's. A rickety, gilded fossil of wealth.

"Here comes Parker," Burns says. "Gabe, ask her to the dance."

"Why don't you?" Gabe asks back.

"Come on," Burns says. "She's a man."

Chase tells him to shut up.

Burns pretends to be hurt. "Didn't mean to insult your *girl*friend."

While once primarily flight or fight, lunch has turned into a meeting place for Noah, Greg, Burns, Chase, Nikki, Parker, and Gabe. The dynamics aren't simple, obviously, or copasetic. Things were more stable when Burns was just a diversion, an entertainer, a halftime show. He used to be a loaded weapon they directed at other tables. But he somehow gained leverage in the group, partly by sucking Noah into his shenanigans, and could now speak his filthy mind without censors.

Nikki and Parker sit down. Whatever guys say in private about Nikki, no one plays hardball with her in public anymore. Just as no one ever mentions Laine. No one goes near the Crash Test Bet at all, as if to invoke the energy of that fiasco is to implicate oneself in it.

Noah asks Nikki as she sits down: "So, who do you think should get lucky with me?"

Nikki scoffs. "You are so confused, dear boy."

No table is a safe haven today from the emotionally gory Valentine's Day Rose tradition, which started this morning and lasts till the Valentine's Day dance. Though this stuff usually tapers off after fourth grade, at Wellington the Rose tradition is strong. Checking one's mailbox to see who, if anyone, sent a rose or, more important, an invite to the formal, is a bloody experience. Virginities have been lost with the turn of a mail key.

Chase's mind is fixed on the rose crushed in his inside pocket. He's sure the person responsible is sitting here.

Burns barks: "It's so *stupid*. This *retarded* Wellington tradition. Are we still in nursery school?"

"Yo, let me guess. No one's sent you flowers, have they, Burns?" Greg asks.

Parker says: "Valentine's Day is just a way to sell chocolates. And Martha Stewart gets to pull out her red glitter—"

"Sounds like Park is batting ole goose egg on the roses as well," Noah interrupts.

"As a matter of fact, Parker has plenty of admirers," Nikki sticks up. "She just doesn't kiss and tell, like you pervs."

"Okay. Whatever, Nik. Can we get back to me?" Noah shifts the attention.

Burns gets a look of malice in his small eyes. "Too bad Mary Love-her-tits isn't still around. You could score with a redhead—"

"Cue to leave," Parker says, cramming the last bit of peanut-butter-and-honey sandwich in her mouth.

"Bon appétit," Nikki says.

"Seriously, guys." Burns pouts. "She had a nice rack, admit it."

As Parker leaves, she looks back at Chase, and he's looking after her. She turns around just in time to avoid walking into a pillar.

"Chase, what's your plan, bro?" Noah continues.

"Funny you should ask, Noah." Chase pulls the crumpled rose from his Brooks Brothers coat and tosses it across the table at Noah. "From Schuyler Covington. Who wants me to go with her to the Valentine's formal. You know anything about this, Ashton?" Chase stares, gauging Noah's guilt or innocence.

"Dude, I had nothing to do with this." Chase has seen Noah's poker face during sprat games and it's a tough read.

"Are you serious, Dobbs?" Burns picks up the note. "Actually, it looks like a chick's handwriting. That's balls if *she's* doing the inviting."

Chase's stare remains on Noah, still convinced he's the one behind the note.

Noah looks away from Chase. "Speak of the devil."

Schuyler approaches with a red cafeteria tray, in a Tracy Feith dress and Chloe gold-buckle boots.

Burns, back turned to Schuyler, continues: "If that shit is real, Dobbs, you better get ready to *work*, my friend, 'cause I heard she's a real cougar." Burns makes his hands into claws and hisses.

Greg, facing Schuyler, shoots Burns a look, but it's too late. Silence as Schuyler hovers. She looks at the rose and then at Chase. "So, whatcha think, buddy?"

But Chase can't breathe. He somehow says "okay."

"Okay? It's just okay?" Schuyler cocks her hip, now leaning against the table, laughing at him. "God, you kill me."

"I mean, yes, that sounds cool," Chase manages. "I'll go with you. Sure."

"That's more like it, mister. So come by my dorm beforehand. We'll meet in the common room. I've got par-tay fay-*vors* for us." Schuyler lifts her tray and sips from the straw in her cardboard chocolate milk container, tawny bangs in her cat eyes.

"Sounds good."

"Okay. I'll let you all get back to whatever it is you all do. See ya Saturday." Schuyler spins and heads toward another table in the middle of the room.

Even Burns is speechless.

6

This semester Parker's job—since all students on financial aid have jobs—is to erase all the classroom boards and stock the pens and erasers. She moves from room to room, as the sun blazes on the ice-crusted horizon outside the windows.

In the science building, she erases formulas and equations. Fish in tanks glow in the dark. She erases centuries of events from the history classrooms. In English classrooms she removes phrases, sentence diagrams, authors' names. Some class has been studying Donne. She erases lines from a love poem.

Chase, where are you? Are you going to ask me or not?

Parker knows *she* could ask *him*, in theory. She even wonders sometimes why she can be honest and straightforward in most situations, but cannot say what she wants in this case. She can barely look him in the eye. It makes her hate herself a little bit. Her dumb mouth won't open; it cannot say certain words.

Chase hasn't been able to crack open a book. His father's lectures have been shredded into strips. The hypothesizing and scheming by his crew about tonight's dance has his brain zooming in twenty directions. They've smoked themselves to death, almost, hiding in the third-floor bathroom after hours, exhaling into the ceiling vent, going over strategy.

One or two fingers? If she goes down on you do you have to return the favor? Do you have to go down first?

After frantically searching the dorm with no luck, Chase stands alone in the infirmary's waiting room, dreading the moment ahead. He's praying for Nurse Jones, the oh-so-sweet, senile, gray-haired nurse who's been known to give out Red Cards for sneezing, and also to wear her pantyhose to work backward, seam in front. When Chase sees a flash of red hair through the reception window, his skin goes pale.

Nurse Sinclair's reputation precedes her as she turns the corner. Part saint and part sinner, she's famous for *not* giving Red Cards unless you're actually vomiting on her shoes, and she's notorious for selling meds on the side. Her old middleman is now on semester abroad in Barcelona, and Burns has supposedly inherited the role. Chase has heard the rumors, but all he is sure of at the moment is that her five-foot-two frame and dark red hair reminds him of Nurse Ratched from *One Flew Over the Cuckoo's Nest*.

"Can I help you, son?" she asks in monotone.

"Umm. I think so." Chase fidgets with his tie.

"Are you sick?"

"No. I'm fine." Chase is flustered by the nurse's puzzled expression. "I mean, someone told me the infirmary gives out condoms."

"You heard correct. Stay right there," she commands.

Where is she going? Chase starts to panic. *Is she going to get a teacher?*

After a few moments, Nurse Sinclair reappears. "Here you are." She hands Chase a box of Trojan condoms and a pamphlet entitled: *Safe Sex for Dummies*. "Read the pamphlet."

Chase thanks her and bolts for the door but the nurse's voice spins him around.

"Good for you for coming to the infirmary, Mr. Dobbs." Chase is shocked she knows his name. The nurse is smiling. "It takes guts, but it's the smart thing to do, kiddo." Chase can't help but smile in return, embarrassed. *God, do I get a gold star? I think this is the first compliment the school's ever given me.* But basically he's grateful to her, and he walks back into the cold with his coat wide-open, the sun hitting his chest.

Chase is cutting through the art building, and sees Parker working in minimal light at an easel. Paint on her hands, a smudge of orange on her nose, Iggy Pop on the radio.

"What are you doing?" he asks, wondering why she's not getting dressed for the dance.

"Painting," she answers, pushing her glasses up with her wrist to avoid getting paint on them. She can't help but feel a flutter in her stomach. Even though most of her has given up on his asking, some piece of her believes that's why he's here.

"I can see that," he says. "But shouldn't you be getting into your ballgown?"

"What ballgown?" she asks, perplexed.

"That's a figure of speech, Park. I mean, shouldn't you be getting ready for the party?"

She looks back to the painting. "Nah. I dunno." *Christ, what am I supposed to say?*

"You'd rather hide out and protest the whole thing and make *art*," he says sarcastically.

"I don't know what I want to do," she says, making little sense but needing to be available if he asks her to go, but protected in case he's not about to ask. She holds her breath, but instead he picks up an envelope jammed with photos. He asks what they're for.

"It's this project. It's an autobiographical painting, like, based on my life. We're supposed to use a photograph."

"May I?" he asks, holding them.

She squirms, pushes up her glasses again, and looks at him with those frank eyes, then shrugs.

There's one of her at maybe eight or nine in a yellow bathing suit under a waterfall.

"It looks cold," he says.

"It was." She smiles. "I was screaming."

Her mouth is in fact wide-open in the picture, palms up to catch the torrent. Hair slicked down like wet silk. Eyes closed in an expression of painful joy.

A photo of her in Vietnam sitting at a table, the hut's door open behind her to a tangle of green. Her little brother sitting next to her, looking up with big eyes, and glasses of milky tea next to a bowl of noodles. Parker explains that her family backpacks, staying in hostels, the kids even taken out of school sometimes. They've explored Mexico, Thailand, Spain, New Zealand.

A shot of her in overalls in a field with sheep, smiling that little girl smile. Parker points to the sheep in the background with the handle of her brush, says her mom used to spin yarn from the wool, then make sweaters for the family.

"Are you serious?" Chase asks.

"Oh, yes. We were *that* family."

He looks closer at her grin; she looks like she owns the field and is content with those animals, with their *Ws* for mouths and their dumb, trusty heads. Her hands grasp her own suspenders, and those fingers look long, even then.

There's a baby picture, and Chase asks: "Is this you?"

She nods, a blush pinking her cheeks. The shot is blurry, and in it she's not laughing or crying; she's just being a baby. In a cloth diaper, she's cradled in the arm of a man with long, dark hair and a huge beard. Her father. He's standing in front of a roughhewn barn, against which leans an old motorcycle. A rusty water pump on the left. A gray sky of thick clouds, a long, open horizon.

It's amazing, Chase thinks. *If anything, she's more of a mystery now.* Seeing someone's childhood in photographs should solve questions, but instead it provokes an awareness of how much life she's lived somewhere else, how much experience she's had, the houses and hostels she's known, the lambs and vegetable gardens and mountains, the school days and Canadian nights, the handmade sweaters.

Other students' paintings, in various stages of completion, are leaned against the wall. But Chase likes hers the best. The painting she's doing now is from a photo of her curled in the back of an RV, in someone's sheepskin jacket. And she's transposed herself so that she's now curled in a cage of bunnies, and she's the same size as them. She's lying in her own rabbit fur jacket, eyes closed in sleep.

"Is this a portrait of dorm life?" he jokes. "Skinning the other girls or something?"

She actually considers this but shakes her head. "Shit, I have no idea what it means. I'm just painting it, and then I'll figure it out."

He surreptitiously examines her face for honesty, and finds nothing but. A piece of the Parker puzzle falls into place. He's always believed she was designing a persona, was doing and wearing and saying everything according to some color-by-numbers freak blueprint. It occurs to him now she's working by instinct.

She realizes he's looking at her strangely, and her heart beats so loudly it actually affects her hearing.

"Well," he says slowly, smiling ruefully at her. "I've got to head."

"Oh, you do?" she says, her mouth dry enough to impede her words.

"Got to pick up my date. Going to this thing with Schuyler, how insane is that?"

They talk a bit more, wrap things up, he closes the door behind him. All very civil, except Parker is present for none of it. He drop-kicked her out of the stadium with that news, and some autopilot part of her took over the small talk.

She lets the studio get dark after that. Lets the twilight spill over the room, seep into her. She absorbs it.

"Hey, Nik—what do you think of this?" Chase busts out of his room to the common room to show his ensemble. Chase's attempt to dress up: His cords are baggy, his one nice jacket short on his arms, his Dogtown and Z-Boys retro surfer hair combed, the laces of his blue Sperry shoes actually tied for once.

"I think you look like a sixteen-year-old virgin." Nikki slouches on the couch and sips the Gatorade vodka Noah stirred up in his room.

"You serious? Get your ass in here and help then." Chase ambles back to his room, annoyed.

"I can't. What if Halliday comes out?"

"Please, the guy's probably bombed on sherry or some shit, watching reruns of *24*."

Nikki enters Chase's room where Gabriel's doing sit-ups in his boxers. Gabe's face goes white.

"Oh. Sorry, Gabe. Should have warned you that a *fee*-male was on the way." Chase tosses Gabriel a T-shirt as he lies on the floor.

Nikki digs through Chase's closet. "Here." She tosses clothes onto Chase's bed. "Just throw the light cords on with the Travota coat and this old preppy tie. You don't need to look dressed up. It's Schuyler, for chrissakes."

79

"Are you sabotaging me?" Chase kids.

But Nikki gives back an icy look. "I should be. I don't even know why you're doing this."

"Going with Schuyler, you mean?" Chase asks defensively. "I'm just messing with her head."

"Riigghhttt," Nikki says derisively.

The door bangs open. Nikki tries to jump into the closet but only manages to get behind the bed.

"*Introducing*: the prettiest nigga in the world." Greg strolls in wearing a white suit, striped green shirt, Gucci shades, no tie. "Shit, I make Usher look like Sam Cassell with an outfit like this."

"Jesus, dude. You scared the shit out of me," Chase says, pulling Nikki out from behind the bed.

"My fault. Didn't know you all had it like that." He laughs and gives Nikki a wink.

"Easy, G. She was helping me get ready for Schuyler."

"Hope she gave you a shot o' Penicillin."

Chase gives Greg a once-over; he's been giving Chase a hard time, elbowing him with little comments here and there, about going with Schuyler. Greg casually dances toward Gabriel's desk. He reaches behind the back leg of the table for a Snapple bottle.

"If you have something to say, Greg . . . ," Chase warns.

"Yeah, I do. I know you ain't going out with that crazy bitch sober." Greg swigs and passes the bottle off to Chase.

"Hard to believe you're going out with her, period." Nikki smiles meanly at Chase and sips her drink. "And you're going to buy that girl a *meal*?"

"I'm *not* going to dinner with her. Just meeting her at the dorm."

"She'll probably have you suffocating in the vice-grip of her thighs by nine." Nikki takes another pull.

"Whoa. Quiet down, Nik." Burns busts through the threshold. "First of all, *that would be awesome*. I would eat three meals a day off that girl's sponge cake. Our boy here has a chance to take down Wellington's most lovely sex kitten." He turns his attention to Chase. "Question one: Did you beat off earlier?"

"What?"

"Because if you didn't I would strongly consider running to the bathroom for a mental challenge. Don't leave one in the chamber with this girl. Anything less than stellar and you'll become that ass-bag from *American Pie*."

The group holds back their laughter in case of faculty. Chase doesn't laugh. He grabs the Snapple bottle and gulps. *These people need to shut up or I'm going to have a full-scale panic attack.*

"Thattaboy. Get bombed and sprinkle a little blow on your tip and you should be rumbling for days." Burns slaps Chase on the back; two old bachelors at some hotel bar. "Always think to yourself, *What would Jack Nicholson do?*"

The bad cocktail burns, and Chase belches iced-tea-lighter-fluid. He tries to go where Burns is pointing him. Because why should he feel bad about any of this? Everyone likes to condemn Schuyler behind her back, *way* behind her back, but if she's in the vicinity, their knees quake.

"I'm getting in the shower," he says, pissed at everyone.

That Crash Test thing, that wasn't engineered by Schuyler alone. A lot of people put in their two cents. Laine didn't end up barefoot on a snowy roof because someone put a gun to her head and forced her up those stairs. And God knows, Nikki brought all the taunting upon herself by acting like a manic Vegas showgirl with a Long Island accent.

Chase hasn't bought an orchid for Schuyler's wrist. He didn't get his cummerbund out of the closet. He didn't splash aftershave on his baby-smooth face. The only primping he's doing is to try to convince himself, as he stares at the dirty tiles of the shower stall and lets water slide down his limp cock, that he hasn't signed up to spend V Day with the devil herself. It's an A-for-effort kind of process.

Parker's hanging out with Aya, Lizzie Jane, and Esther in Aya's room, eating caramel popcorn and drinking soda, looking through dirty personals online. They pore over photographs of what's being offered: *tie me up, hit me, love me, use me.* The photographs are graphic, close-ups taken in mirrors with digital cameras, faces left out of the frame. In the corners of the shots, a dirty stuffed animal, a bed with no sheets.

Parker doesn't get involved; it's too depressing. She lounges on Aya's bed, pawing through candy hearts. *Be mine. Dream dreamer. I'm yours.*

Why can't she stop thinking of him? He's such an asshole! She believes she hates him, as she pops a heart in her mouth. With his long gold hair, those rumpled clothes that hang off him but stay on, everything holding gallantly by a thread, magically. *Jesus.* The heat of his arm on her shoulders, her shoulders practically turning red like the coils in a space heater. Except this ache, this heat, this need gets welded with hatred right now—because that arm's on another girl's shoulders.

Small groups, shrieking as someone almost falls but is caught by another, pick their frozen way from dorms to the main hall where the Valentine's dance is held. True cold sears the face, numbs the fingertips *through* gloves. When you inhale, all your nostril hairs freeze and become like straight pins, stiff and sharp, and then when you breathe out hot air, they melt. Girls walk to the main building in parkas over formal dresses. Guys skid over the ice in loafers.

For all the build-up of a holiday dance, it's just another

Saturday night in disguise. People do dress up, and a handful of out-of-towners (sweethearts from back home) who are willing to come to the icy village of Glendon have arrived, and everyone is less reserved on the dance floor. On the tables are cheap cupcakes, the icing spilled haphazardly over them, and there's a bowl of neon-red punch. It's not even spiked.

Schuyler and her crew keep disappearing into a bathroom. The older crew that parties leaves Lower-forms out in the cold, Chase has noticed. When there's so little to go around, materials are hoarded, and people get shady. It's such a lonely thing to begin with, partying in these big, cold buildings, when your life can be upended if you get caught, and the secrecy makes it even lonelier. The girls are like ghosts, floating through empty rooms to sniff their drugs and slam their shots in dangerous silence. These adventures have none of the heat or love that happens at a real party.

Chase tracks down Greg. He's tucked in a dark corner of the main hall, curled into a couch with Caroline Camper, and it looks like they're holding hands in the shadows and whispering, so Chase moves on.

In the snack bar his crew holds court. He watches from outside as Noah does an impression of someone. Nikki laughs. They look somewhat banged up.

"Hey there, stranger. I was wondering where you disappeared to." Schuyler reappears and gives Chase a kiss.

Definitely took a shot. Thank God she didn't puke. Chase can hear Burns screaming "Beat it down" as he walks Schuyler, who has a slight weave to her steps now, back to the dance floor.

Ever since he first laid eyes on her, Chase has thought Schuyler looked like someone he knew. Suddenly he realizes who. He'd even passed her when he was home for Christmas and not realized: It was the mannequin in the Mayfair Boutique, one of the oldest stores in Charleston, where every mother has a charge account. She's in the window, with dust in the corners of her painted blue eyes, but with the exact same tawny hair and shiny shoulders. The thin smile, the unflappable confidence—she'd been staring down passersby walking on the cobblestones of King Street for the past forty years. Looking at them, men and women and kids alike, and sending out the message, with a possible twitch of the lips—*You* will *love me.*

After ten minutes of aggressive grinding, Chase can't continue. He turns away and readjusts himself, uncomfortable from Schuyler pushing her ass into him and wrapping his hands around her thighs.

"Are you *trying* to make this embarrassing?" he asks desperately.

"Aw, don't be embarrassed," she says, as if comforting a child. "You want to leave? I have a master key."

Chase shrugs. "I'll do whatever."

Schuyler whispers in his ear. "I think you wanna leave."

Whatever combination of pills and booze she's taken makes Schuyler into a toy programmed by a factory worker, her eyes glazed, her functions automatic.

His pants are down and her underwear is off before Schuyler can even lock room 412 of the Latin wing. She lies back on the table and pulls up her dress. It's already nine forty-five and Chase is relieved there's not too much time. Schuyler guides his hand to her as he rips down his pants. The air is filled with the faint smell of chalk. A stone bust of someone glows in the corner.

She whispers hoarsely in his ear. Chase reaches for his pants and grabs a condom. His mind is racing. *Calm down. Calm down.*

The motion is slow. Her legs wrapped around him, he stands above her. She moans softly, and he catches her staring at him. Her eyes seem mischievous, as if she knows a secret about him. *I think it's been about a minute. This is pathetic. Oh shit.*

He comes quietly, withholding his pleasure. He keeps pushing for a minute more and stops. In a moment of pure genius, he stands back.

"Holy shit. I think the condom broke." He turns his back to her and pretends to inspect the condom, ripping it off and tossing it in the trashcan.

"I'm on the Pill." She reaches, but he breaks away from her grip.

"I can't do that shit. Plus I lost my hard-on 'cause of this commotion and we have Check In in ten minutes."

"You what?" Schuyler inspects her body with dumb awe, like a volunteer who was sawed in half by a magician and is now amazed to be whole again at the end of the trick.

"I, you know, lost it."

Schuyler is defeated and lays back on the table in purposeful protest, her half nakedness now an affront to him, an accusation, and he doesn't look at her. "Well *that* was boring," she says.

"Can we maybe meet tomorrow for round two?"

"You're kidding, I hope."

"Guess I am then. . . . Let's get out of here."

Chase waits for Schuyler in silence while she puts on lip gloss like an automaton, remaking her mouth, reactivating herself after some sort of oblivion they just experienced. He tries to hold her hand but she pulls it away from his.

The shower is four feet deep when Chase arrives. His boys in bathing suits, Gatorades in hand, swimming around their makeshift bath. On Cadwallader 2 the communal showers have a wall surrounding them. For years boys have simply duct-taped cardboard to the entryway and filled the shower to create a midnight pool.

Greg spots Chase and shouts: "I know you killed it. I saw your goofy ass on the dance floor trying to hide your dick."

"A gentleman never tells, boys. Luckily my father is the only gentleman in the family." Chase puts a fist in the air and announces with pride: "Schuyler Covington is now a woman."

Chase takes a running start and dives in the pool fully clothed.

Burns hands out Stacker 2 pellets, calling the yellow and black capsules "queen bees." For the next half hour Chase does a much enhanced play-by-play of the night. He includes dirty talk and throws in his open invitation for tomorrow, minus her response, of course. Burns excuses himself to go beat off twice. The boys of Cadwallader 2 smoke cigarettes and take shots. It's an upside down Valentine's Day, everyone giddy with disappointment.

At the end, Burns is curled up in the corner of the tiled space, passed out. Empty whippet canisters, discarded like shotgun shells, lie around him, glittering. Chase can practically see hearts and bluebirds and stars circling and popping effervescently above Burns's head. His briefs are soaked with water and translucent. It's amazing to Chase how the kid is never satisfied, and has to chase the extremes, the darkness, the lights-out in his own head.

* * *

Parker's found some privacy in the bathtub room on the fourth floor that no one uses except to smoke. She rolls a cigarette in honey-dipped paper, lights it, and unlocks the ancient window. The seam is clotted with dead bees. She blows smoke at the orange moon.

I could have asked him before she did; I could have showed him I wanted to be asked. Don't be shy, they say. That's the same as saying "Don't be yourself, Parker, don't be who you are." Screw you. This is what I do, I watch, I wait, I see things other people don't see sometimes. In this stupid, aggressive culture, they seem to think that's a crime.

The funny thing is she doesn't even know who "they" are. She doesn't know who she's arguing with. She sits on the edge of the tub, a relic from a different era when students took baths. She flicks ashes into the drain. Her thinking swings back to hating him, hating him for asking Schuyler at all, or saying yes to her or however it happened. The girl is *nasty*, and he should have shown more character. Or any character.

She wants to claw open the wall, draw blood from the plaster. *That's it. I'll close myself off. Thank God I didn't tell anyone I thought he was going to ask me. That's all I would need, a cherry on top.*

For some sad reason, she thinks of Emily Dickinson's poems, found all rolled up and tied with ribbons in a drawer when she'd died. Work she'd not been able to get out to the world. Understandable to be afraid, to hold on to secrets. But pathetic to tie them up in pink silk. *And pathetic of me to think about them right now.*

Blue would say: *She should have burned them.*

If it wouldn't cause a commotion, Parker would howl like a wolf right now. A roar burns in her throat.

Later, Chase lies in bed, nerves jangling from the diet pill he took and from jumping around. Each time he tips into sleep, his mind comes up with a kaleidoscope of images. He sees his elementary-school classroom with construction-paper hearts taped to the windows. Schuyler's wet mouth, the wand of her gloss as she runs it over her lips again and again. Her tongue flicking out like a valentine. His grand-mother in her garden wearing gloves and white sunglasses, her hand reaching out with shears to snip a stem; the red rose falls to the ground in slow motion. The berry of Schuyler's nipple. Cutting out gold trim at his second-grade desk, the folded card he's making blank so far. Laine's blue eyes standing out in a face darkened by an unfathomable shadow. His child hand reaching for the Elmer's bottle, the glue spurting out—

He sits up.

Parker lies in bed on her back, facing the ceiling, looking up there for sleep to come down on her. Charlotte is already crashed out, her cream and brown houndstooth coat put away, her black hair ribbon rolled up and stowed in the silver monogrammed box. Her peachy cheeks damp and freshly Noxzemaed, her wet eyes closed.

Oh, Charlotte. Parker has poked and prodded and peered and stirred and provoked and invoked—in her Parker way— and has discovered no contours of soul there yet. Like poking a dead bird with a twig; you go on doing it long after you're sure the bird is gone. She always assumed that because Charlotte grew up with a harelip, she might know things, understand life, *get it*. But instead she's not bitter nor blasé; she just walks around with her hand cupped over the scar, as though about to tell someone a secret. She's cool as milk.

Charlotte's tobacco-brown empire-waist dress hangs now on the closet door: not in triumph nor in defeat. Just a symbol of having participated. A dark stamp of completion. *Valentine's Day: done. Dancing: accomplished. Curfew: achieved.* She's breathing now the way she does when she's deep in sleep, barely audible except for little coughs. Parker lies in her own space, silent, desperate.

She's wearing a violet slip, her own footnote for love today. But the thing instead feels dirty and awful. And she's feeling too bad to get up, tiptoe to find another nightgown.

She slips one hand under the strap, closes her long fingers over her small breast. Cups the other hand over the violet silk between her legs. She's trying to take some mid-night inventory. *What am I?* she thinks in despair, measur-ing herself. *What comprises me, for God's sake, what am I made of?*

Hey, Laine. He's typing in the dark, sweating, but deter-mined. Fuck it, why not. *Wow, I have to admit, I'm a little twisted right now. Long night, long story, you know how it is. But I was trying to sleep, and I just couldn't, right? I just can't. It's Valentine's Day and I wish you were here. I love you.*

Send.

He lies back in bed. He's flooded with weird voltage. He's never said that to anyone. It's like he was taken over by some supernatural Romeo, who'd forced his fingers to hit those keys. He's exhilarated and horrified, but has no regrets. His mind swoops over the miles, the snowy back-yards and streets and hills and homes and woods like a low-flying plane, to where she's asleep, a love letter on fire in her inbox.

7

The combination of February's limitless dark and the aftertaste of Valentine's night with Schuyler, who won't acknowledge him in the halls now, and the lack of response from Laine to his insane e-mail, has sent Chase into a murky, moldy depression. His crew has become as dull as the overused toys of a hyperactive child. His ambitions are stale. If he was barely doing his work before, he's not even keeping up appearances now.

His days are poor reality-TV segments:

1) Rise at seven forty-five A.M. Smell out dirty laundry on floor for the least offensive turtleneck and semibearable socks; check e-mail.

2) Class until three thirty P.M. with a dorm-room nap during lunch; halfhearted, unconsummated jacking off;

scramble to get homework done; check e-mail.

3) Squash practice. Pretend to compete knowing you'll never be more than an alternate this season.

4) Dinner with team at six thirty; check e-mail.

5) Study hall from seven thirty to nine thirty; cram four hours of homework into two hours.

6) Steal a smoke with Burns in the shower during nine thirty to ten break.

7) Check In at ten. Video games on illegal TV till passing out.

Whenever Chase feels his seams breaking, instead of pulling it together, he obsesses harder and stronger over any current and primary obsessions. That's always been his style, whether he was a kid consumed with desire for a Tonka truck, or a sixteen-year-old who spends hours on a certain blond girl's azure eyes.

Winter break is four days away; if Chase can keep it together, he'll be in Virginia with Reed, tearing it up. Granted, Reed complained over Christmas about Chase visiting, but Chase knows Reed wants to show off his new life.

He swan dives into his Laine fantasy even though the power of the fantasy is getting weak, since it's been so long since he saw her, and he's been using the memory without restraint. But finally he gets an e-mail back, which helps. Although she doesn't quite make it to the finish line of saying *I love you*, she does tell him her parents are now trying to get her into another school, but she's trying to come back to Wellington largely *because of you, Chase*. It's definitely an e-mail that took many hours to compose. He sees her writing it in some third-story room at an antique desk, gazing out the window at Greenwich's maze of hedges.

How cool would it be to take her to UVA this weekend? Reed would be jealous for once. Reed with his corn-blond square hair and beauty mark on the cheek, Reed who was *born* filled out, and never acted "too sensitive" according to his father, never moody, never theatrical—those being Chase's repeat crimes. Reed, who dated a string of skinny blondes from good families. Reed, who talked slow and a bit lazy but struck fast. Chase never even saw it coming till he felt hot skin on his face and thought—*I've been hit*.

He even dreams of introducing Laine to his father. Like offering a gold cup of ram's blood to a god. *What the hell? It's crazy.* Some girls, you want them to teach you things in the dark. Some girls you hang tough with, smoke and drink with, never touch. And other girls, you want to make sure no one gets near them so you can marry them the day you're legal. That's how he feels about Laine: desperate to save her for himself.

"Chase, are you listening?"

Chase and Parker's attempt to pass the first big

95

Limnology test is elaborate. Frederick's midterm is planned for Tuesday and so they're holed up in a study room dank with hundreds of hours of studying over the years. On the table, diagrams and vocabulary lists and practice quizzes, the textbook open to a juicy photograph of larvae.

"Sorry, I'm busy admiring your Necco Wafers." Chase points at the roll of candy. "Who the hell eats those? They belong in a museum."

"I got them yesterday in a care package," she says curtly, but hopefully not too curtly. She promised herself to be civil with him and to keep her voice from shaking.

"And who still gets care packages?" Chase smiles. "You're very old-school, Parker."

"Oh, give it up," she says scornfully. "I saw your mother sent you ginger cookies the other day."

"Let me get one." Chase reaches across the table. "Chase needs some sugar, Doc. I'm crashing."

Parker holds up a wafer, waving it in his face. "You want this?"

Chase plays along, folding his hands in prayer. Parker can't help but laugh. His long hair summons ideas of Jesus, the candy being a communion wafer. *Damnit!* Why can't she stick to being short with him?

When she was little, everyone thought it was hysterical to watch her ride this rocking horse her dad built. She would hold the reins to make the horse rock, but the plaything had its own mind, and she often fell off. Parker was just clumsy, off-beat, bad at working the toy. So people watched and laughed at this little girl so profoundly out of control and backward.

This is how she feels now; her head is trying to ride her heart, and the heart is out of control.

"Here's the deal." Parker tries to get serious. "I'm going to hold up a flashcard and if you get the answer right, then I'll give you a wafer. Okay?"

"That's cruel. But go ahead, Cole, I'll be the teacher's pet."

"You're corny."

Parker and Chase smile. Chase hasn't been this comfortable with a girl since before sixth grade. More specifically, since the night he saw Justin Manner's dog-eared and dilapidated *Hustler* in the glare of a flashlight in a tent. Everything changed in that moment.

Parker shuffles her deck, pulls a card. She reads: "*Cultural eutrophication*," each letter written in a different shade of green; Parker manages to turn science class into art.

"Okay, Dobbs. Please tell me five negative effects of cultural eutrophication on Lake Dory." Parker holds the card close to her chest.

Chase bites his lip. "Let's see. Reduced water transparency, an increase in algae, fish kills, a rapid shift in the lake species." Chase pauses.

"You need one more." Parker holds up four fingers.

"I know. Cool your jets. And Parker not being able to bathe in it or fill up her hippie Nalgene water bottle."

"That's six, jackass." Parker slings a Necco Wafer at Chase's chest.

After a round of flash cards, Chase leans back and sighs. Then he pokes his head out of the library study room and closes the door. "Adderal makes me want to smoke. You mind if I pack?" He pulls out a tin of Skoal mint and beats it in between middle and index fingers.

"No, it's fine. Let's take a break. Can I bum one?"

"Nothing sexier than a lady who dips."

Parker uses Chase's empty Teany bottle, a dribble of brown spit on her chin. Chase dabs it with the cuff of his corduroy shirt. She blushes, as she's always uncoordinated with him. It's like her hands go rigid and useless as a doll's. And she's never sure if words will actually come out of her mouth; she practically does a microphone check before she meets up with him.

But when she does start talking, she can't stop.

Most people Chase knows talk about other people. They talk about how other people look, or who likes or hates who else, or who's rich and poor. They talk about how fucked up the school is, how fucked up the teachers are, how home is so much better, full of freedom and booze and life.

Parker is slow to start up but if he asks her enough questions, she talks about how weird it is to listen to a surf report on a Venice Beach radio station streaming on her computer while snow is coming down outside her window. Parker talks about how in restaurants in Greece you go back into the kitchen and talk to the cook about what you want or should have for dinner. Parker talks about Lucien Freud, the painter and son of Sigmund, and *The Perfumed Garden*, a fifteenth-century Arabic book on love, and bluegrass, and the price of oil, and owls, and snuff films.

When she gets excited about whatever she's discussing, she adjusts those horn-rims more often than she has to. She looks at a place above Chase's head, as if there's a written note on everything she ever wanted to tell him. She pulls her dark hair with one pale hand, smiles while she explains the things she thinks about.

When she points out that they need to keep studying, Chase tells her that he's more scared than ever he won't pass this class. They talk about his ADD, and it turns out that Parker's parents are on Mr. Dobbs's side; they don't put much stock in the diagnosis.

"How can I explain?" Chase asks, slightly exasperated. How can he make anyone understand how facts and figures come rushing at him, like soldiers on a field, and he can't fight them all, so he retreats, and fights none.

"Let's just keep waging small battles, Dobbs. Don't take it all on at once."

By the end of the session, they're back in that close and easy place where they were before Valentine's Day. Parker is mad at herself for this, and euphoric, and amazed. She's never been split down the middle before.

She has to ask before they go. They're standing at the door to the library, about to leave the golden rooms for the icy, bitter walk to their own dorms. "I meant to ask, Chase. How was Valentine's, your date, you know?"

He's wrapping his scarf around his neck. "Ugh. Biggest mistake of my life."

"Can't say I'm surprised," she says boldly.

"Thanks a lot, kid," he says with faux bitterness, and waves good-bye as they part.

Biggest mistake. Biggest mistake. Parker keeps saying it to herself. It's a great love story in two words.

For Chase, Algebra I is a carefully written system of torture. The textbook pretends to be a learning tool, but on its pages are pronged and booby-trapped formulas and diagrams that leave quills in the skin after he's fought them. French, at least he likes speaking the language, letting those grand phrases roll off the tongue. But he sure as hell can't remember how to *spell* those grand phrases. And if someone put a gun to his head he wouldn't be sure if the sky was feminine or masculine; *it's blue*. He's got Ballast again for English, but they're reading Dante's *Inferno*, and for some reason he can't get any of the material straight, whereas normally understanding books comes naturally to him.

Once they get past the facts, though, and into the ideas, Chase loves that class. The *Oxford English Dictionary* on the antique podium. Ballast's manic hieroglyphics on the marker board. The outside world, with its icy hills rolling up to the classroom, meeting the warm window, the hand of a fir tree pressed to the glass as if to feel the heat, its blue needles splayed. But he has trouble explaining why he loves it so much, just as he can't explain why the other stuff is impossible.

Parker's mind is quirky. Not traditionally left- or right-brained. Her intellect is a town with roads and intersections no one can navigate but her. Both her parents are professors, PhDs, and have taken their share of peyote—especially Genevieve, her mom. Genevieve can prove any-one wrong, even if they're right. Her dad, Ben, can draw a map of Africa with his eyes closed, down to the last town. Both their offices are in the house, and the house is asleep sometimes during the day and lit up and awake at night with work. At one A.M. her parents might emerge from their offices, eyes red from study, throw a record on the turntable, and start to roast a chicken while sipping straw-berry wine.

Parker can memorize. She can synthesize. She can artic-ulate. Parker reads sheet music. Parker knows some John

Berryman by heart. Prime numbers, to her, are elegant. The periodic table is beguiling. Picasso is familiar.

If she has a flaw, it's that she gets lost in it all. She once stood by Ben in a field at home, after hiking. They had unlaced their boots and were sitting on a boulder, drinking water under a cold misty sun. Her dad said something like: *Park, this is infinity in a way. Think about it. All these systems are snaking out from this spot. That hawk is looking to kill a mouse, who just ate the seeds off a blackberry bush. And that food chain continues in both directions. The structures of this world, and our bodies, and the molecular architecture of this boulder. The books written on each one of those topics. The thoughts human beings have thought about those books. The paintings and photographs made of this landscape. This physical place, which you would believe to be finite, is not so, is it?*

The snow on the peak, that will come down the stream, and will go back up as rain, Parker added.

Ben had smiled at her. *Rain.*

And Parker did feel all that; she could sit anywhere and it might take her hours to get her bearings. To sort through the infinity of any one moment.

Put these two minds together, Parker's and Chase's, and their Limnology test is conquered that Tuesday by each one, separately. They walk out, knowing they passed with flying colors, and Chase treats them to chocolate milk shakes at the snack bar. Parker puts the whole *White*

Album on the jukebox, and they loiter, slouching, laughing for hours.

Chase is lying facedown on his pillow as Gabriel enters the room humming.

"How'd it go?" Gabriel smacks Chase on the back of his head as he turns toward his closet.

Chase mumbles into his pillow.

"Lift your head up when you speak."

"I said, I *fucking passed.*"

"You serious?"

"There is no conceivable way I failed." Chase rolls over and sighs. "I don't think I've ever said that sentence before." He notices Gabriel packing. "You leaving now?"

"Yeah. Burns has a car coming to take him home so he's dropping me at my hotel."

"When are you heading out?"

"Fifteen minutes, I think. Car's out front. When are you leaving?"

"I take off from Hartford at three tomorrow. Everyone else is out of here today. I'm going to be solo on campus. Reed's busy till tomorrow, but who gives a shit; thank God I'm not going home. My dad will murder me when he sees my other midterm grades."

"I thought you were doing better this semester."

"I keep thinking I am because I spend more time in the

library, but that's not exactly sufficient." Chase stares at the ceiling. "Who cares, right?"

Gabriel is conspicuously quiet. He would never do less than a hundred percent on his work. He slides both suitcases to the door and nods at Chase.

"What?" Chase stares back coldly.

"Be a good roommate and help me carry this crap, eh?"

Chase smiles and stands up. A few months back, shy Gabriel wouldn't have mustered up a decent good-bye to Chase, and now he's busting his balls.

As Chase lugs Gabriel's Dunhill luggage downstairs he makes fun of his roommate's panache: The muted blue Thom Browne suit is pressed, and after three months of snow his suede loafers are still impeccable. Handkerchief folded into a triangle in coat pocket, silver belt buckle shined. But Chase has respect for it. When Gabe sees his parents, he doesn't casually intend to impress–they *expect* to see a young man.

"Gabe, what are you doing all weekend? You meeting up with Noah and the rest?"

"Not this time. My parents are in town with my sister. We're hosting a dinner at the Met tomorrow. I expect the rest of the time we'll just visit other family. Speaking of, you're definitely coming to my uncle's place in Costa Rica over Spring Break, right?"

"Yeah, man. Can't wait for that." Chase appreciates his

roommate trying to cheer him up for being left behind, but right now Spring Break is a long way off. Plus, to Chase a weekend with family is boring, so he isn't jealous of his plans. Gabriel actually likes it. A stretch S500 Mercedes idles outside Cadwallader. Chase can tell Burns and Noah are already in the car as smoke wafts from a crack in the tinted back window.

"Move kids! Get out the way!" Greg appears with a gym bag and a grin. "Just got a pass from Dean Braden to head out with you all." He throws his arm around Gabriel and Chase: "No school shuttle for Greg."

Greg's pants are pressed and his shirt starched; he looks like a toy soldier. His parents also expect a man when he comes home.

"Unfucking believable," Chase says. "You're headed to the city tonight too?"

Greg nods his head and grins.

Burns rolls down the window and stabs his cigarette against the side of the car. "Will the two minority students get in the car. I don't want to drive back too late after dark with you two in case we get pulled over."

"You're funny," Greg says evenly as he gets in.

Burns begins to roll up the window but spots Chase: "Hey, Dobbs. Try not to pick up any diseases in Charlottesville. Later."

When did Burns become a member of their posse? He

used to be a mascot, a village idiot. Chase watches the white car disappear into the New England dusk. Burns actually freaks him out sometimes. Is the way he stares at girls lewd or homicidal? It's hard to tell. And the guy never seemed to understand that girls could see him staring. He was that unaware of himself.

But Chase is envious of their car ride. Taking shots and sharing butts. Enjoying the high you get when you step foot off campus, headed to a paradise of forbidden things, real and imagined.

Chase packs a dip and works PlayStation in his room. He orders in pizza and throws *Layer Cake* onto his laptop, but doesn't feel like watching it again. He tries out his Laine daydreams, but finds her fuzzy around the edges.

He feels stir-crazy, abnormal, and decides to take a walk. There's a quiet on campus, a silence that comes from the marrow of the buildings. If he cups his hands around his mouth and shouts *hello* into the darkness, he'd get bombarded by Grand-Canyon-level echoes. Faculty are immediately relaxed once students leave—he sees Mr. Grenville and Ms. Pierce on the front lawn in the light of a lamp. He's petting her dog, and they're both laughing. It makes him realize how formal the existence at Wellington is otherwise.

The wind picks up the first layer off the snow, whirls it in crystalline eddies. The crunch of his shoes is loud in the big night. He doesn't walk to the lake, although he's always drawn there, as if the lake is the hot core of this world and it exerts gravity on him. Instead he walks along the periphery of the woods, and up Blading Hill, away from school. At the top, he can see the grounds, sparsely lit tonight, and the lake.

People swear they've seen the ghost of Mary Loverwest. A luminous figure with red hair slipping through black trees. They hear her voice in the wind, breathing hard as she walks, the metal zipper tag of her parka jingling. Someone sees *Mary Wuz Here* scrawled in the snow, but it's gone by the time he drags back a witness. *That's what you get,* Chase thinks, *from a generation breastfed on horror flicks.*

Chase lights a cigarette. The coal stains his hand with orange light. The truth is that he *wishes* Mary would come haunt him. That some undead girl would appear from that grove of darkness, and walk up to him, otherworldly hands in her otherworldly pockets, and they wouldn't be afraid of each other. Chase exhales cold smoke. *Honestly, come talk to me, Mary. There are so many things I would ask you. Questions whose answers you might have by now.* He stands there, ashing into a snow-covered briar patch, casually annoyed—as if he did in fact have a rendezvous with a ghost, and she was just running a few minutes late.

8

Chase arrives with big expectations. He keeps adjusting his clothes on the plane, running his hands through his hair. Watching squares of farmland and clusters of town beneath them. When he lands, he sees Reed's text to meet in baggage claim. But Chase is confused; a guy in a UVA lacrosse hat, white polo shirt, and pleated khakis is holding a sign with his name on it.

"I'm Daniel. I'm here to pick you up."

"Oh." *A pledge.* Chase remembers Reed bitching about his own pledge semester at the Delta house. The errands, the house lore he learned, the raw eggs–or "yume"–he swallowed, during Hell Week. "Thanks for the ride, man."

The Delta house reminds Chase of Charleston mansions that families have lived in for generations, grand in their day but now barely livable. "House proud, cash poor," his dad would say. The missing windows and spray paint on the Delta house take that even further. A brother opens the door.

Thirty guys are seated on benches at wooden tables. It's a rainbow of polo shirts, baseball caps, and corduroy pants. Reed stands and offers Chase his hand; the Dobbs men never hug. At 6'4", Reed's even taller than Chase and has his mother's dark eyes. "Hey, bud. Meet everyone."

The intros are cut short when a voice booms: "Hampton, you think you're the coolest fucking kid in here, right?" Chase sees the voice: older, with a five-o'clock shadow, a Remington camouflage ball cap pulled low over his unibrow, chest hair tufting out of a pink polo shirt, collar up.

Hampton, a short kid standing at the ice cooler, shakes his head, but camo-man continues: "I mean, you brought that hot piece of *ass* to the party last Saturday. Why don't you tell us all what happened when you brought her home that night?"

A voice shouts, "Better be good!"

Hampton pauses: "Umm, not much."

"That sucks, Hampton!" the camo-man screams. A dinner roll smacks Hampton's face. "Put your fucking hand in the icebox. Maybe that will jolt your memory."

Laughter from the tables. Hampton sticks his right hand into the ice.

"Up to your fucking elbow, Hampton!" Another roll, in the gut. "You're going to leave it there until we hear something good. I mean, dick-throbbing good, you hear me!"

Another voice shouts, "Did you give her the Mexican dipstick?" and another, "The dirty Sanchez?"

Hampton is flustered. "Umm yeah, I fingered her and she, like, beat me off."

There's a chorus of boos and "That's weak!"

Reed hurries toward the kitchen and reappears with a metal stockpot, which he puts over Hampton's head.

"Maybe this will jog your memory." Reed hammers the pot with a spoon. After eight or nine whacks, guys pull Reed away.

"That's enough, man," another voice roars. "Dinner's over!"

Up in Reed's room, Chase asks what the hell that was about.

"Relax, it's just a show. That shit is staged." Reed and Chase are playing Tiger Woods PGA Tour on PlayStation. Drive-By Truckers posters and tapestries line the walls.

"I thought you said when you got in, you wouldn't haze."

Reed pauses as he prepares for his next shot. "It wasn't that big of a deal. We all went through it."

"Yeah, but—"

"So Dad tells me you're messing up at school."

"Nah, man. I don't know." Chase thinks. "Wellington is just, I don't know, depressing. I'm just not into it."

"Just not into it," Reed says bitterly. "What have you ever been into, little brother?"

"Easy. It's not like I don't have things going on."

"What does that mean?"

"I mean, school sucks, but whatever, I took Schuyler to the Valentine's Dance. We got fucked up, had a decent time."

Reed grins at the computer screen. "Get out. That's awesome."

Chase has a moment of glory before getting destroyed.

"Schuyler Covington. That's *awesome*," Reed repeats. "I took her to her first Valentine's Dance, if you know what I mean, little brother."

Chase works hard not to drop his joystick. "I knew that."

"She's one of the lucky many who have surrendered to yours truly. I love it, she's getting back at me through you. It's priceless."

Chase pretends to keep playing but he's really remembering the whole Valentine's Dance, except now it's upside down.

Having to stay at Wellington over Long Winter Break is punishment for the detention kids. The other major populations that stay are financial aid and scholarship kids who

111

can't afford to travel and international kids who have too far to go. So the group is spicy. It's a strange ensemble, and a derelict and strangely fun weekend. The grounds are empty, and the buildings grow, expanded by their hollowness. The click of a coin dropped in a marble hall makes an apocalyptic clatter.

Nikki and Parker play Jenga with fish sticks, slouching, talking loudly, and calling attention to how cavernous the dining hall is. Parker makes a homemade milk shake by mushing ice cream with a spoon, and it's too gross to eat.

"Shit, what should we do?" Nikki asks.

Parker shrugs. "Arson? Hacking?"

They play Ping-Pong, which they've never done before because the table is the jurisdiction of seniors. Their game, which isn't great to start, disintegrates into slamming the ball as hard as they can, so that it bounces against the ceiling, rolls into the hall.

"Kill it!" Nikki cheers on Parker who's about to serve.

It's a form of therapy.

"Are we effing losers here, Park?"

"Well, you're trapped in detention and I'm a trapped Canadian. I'd say there's a good chance."

Nikki lobs a forehand serve, disregarding the two-bounce rule, and Parker whiffs.

"What do you think everyone else is up to? Where's your Limno buddy, Chase? Do you think he's dorking out too? Maybe he and Schuyler are doing it on a Ping-Pong table somewhere."

"That's not nice, Nik," Parker says defensively.

"Oh. Since when did you start sticking up for Chase?"

"Chase is at UVA visiting his brother. Plus, I think he learned a lesson with Schuyler. No more psycho older girls."

At the Crusty Wahoo, even before the brothers order beers, two blond girls approach.

"Chase, this is Rosemary and Amy," Reed says as if he owned the joint.

Both girls are dressed in AG low-rise jeans and Calypso tanks with necklaces dangling. "Nice to meet y'all," Rosemary says.

"He's too cute." Amy winks at Reed, and they walk away together.

Rosemary asks if he's coming to UVA next year. Figuring Reed set him up and not wanting to blow it, Chase says maybe, but he's waiting to hear from Princeton.

"Cool. Let's do some shots."

"Wahoo!" Rosemary screams and pounds the first Red Bull/Jägermeister concoction of many. Chase goes along with the routine. After their second bomb, she asks if Reed and him are going out to the Stronghold later. Chase says he thinks so, even though he has no idea what she's talking about, and that she should come along. She says she's planning on it since she's in the Orchids, the sister sorority, she "can go, like, whenever."

On his way to the bathroom, Chase pulls Reed aside.

"She told you about the Stronghold?" Reed looks pissed. "Stupid slut."

"What's the big deal?"

"It's this secret fraternity. Chicks aren't supposed to blab about it. Whatever. We'll roll out in a little while."

On Reed's cue, the group piles into Amy's Range Rover, and they get on, then off the highway, drive a mile down the pitch-black road. A glow through overhanging elm trees in the distance. The Stronghold looks like a medieval castle, complete with tower. People hang on the stone porch, cigarettes illuminating the twenty-five-foot fortress doors and portcullis.

Rosemary pulls him inside. A fire blazes and Jay-Z's "Encore" rattles swords on mahogany walls. Couples grind under a chandelier.

Reed and Amy linger on the dance floor.

After they fill cups at the keg, Rosemary and Chase head up a winding staircase. In a second-floor room, guys huddle around a table, white powder on a framed picture between them. Someone waves at Rosemary.

The third-floor room they enter is dark, barely lit by Tiffany lamps. Once Chase's eyes adjust, he scans photographs taken over many years of serious men in white tuxes and black sashes at the Stronghold.

Rosemary pushes Chase down on a leather couch. "Have you done GHB before?"

"Yeah, a couple times," he lies.

Rosemary pulls out a Mr. Bubbles pink container. "Open sesame."

When the warmth hits, it's in his legs. It picks up the pace through his thighs and stomach, then into his arms and chest. *Okay, don't freak out.* It climbs his spine. *Oh shit, this isn't good.* His body feels fifteen degrees hotter. He takes a pull on his keg cup. *You're fine. You're fine.* Another swig. He smiles and looks at the ceiling and then to Rosemary. *I'm fine.*

Sweat glistens off Rosemary's high cheekbones. *I want to lick her face.* She's complaining about who to bring to the formal. She went to the Phi Gamma cocktail with this older guy who's cool, so she might ask him, but there's this guy in her class who is "so fierce." *Amazing, we've got the same issues.* Chase tells her about Schuyler, Laine, and even Parker. Chase is pretty sure this is the most meaningful conversation he's ever had and when Rosemary asks if he wants another capful, he thinks it's the best idea he's ever heard.

The glow begins again and Chase smiles expectantly.

"You peaking, cutey?" Rosemary slides her hand onto his lap. He tries to say he's never felt better but his words trail. Everything moves in slow motion. Rosemary straddles him and kisses his neck, ears, mouth. Jeans grind corduroys. He slides his hands up her back and likes how her skin is cool. He reaches around to her breasts, which are even cooler.

Her grinding picks up speed and warmth floods his lower body. Chase groans.

"What the fuck are you doing?" Rosemary looks down at Chase's lap.

"What?" Chase sees a stain spreading around his crotch.

Rosemary springs up. "You are not serious." She bolts, walking backward, disoriented, angry.

The next morning, at Bodo's Bagels, Chase nurses the worst hangover in his life with a sesame bagel, veggie cream cheese, and a Coke. He woke up on a couch in the Delta house common room with no clue how he got there. His brother must have dragged him home. He tried to go to his room this morning, but Reed told him to go away. Amy was still in there. He feels his crusted corduroys again, and winces. *Couldn't Reed have had the courtesy to give me a pair of pants?*

Staring at his bagel, Chase daydreams about Mary's funeral back in her hometown, which he's never done before but is compelled now to do. A few of her Wellington friends flew there for it. They said the church was so full, people had to stand on the steps outside, in the freezing cold, as mass was said inside. Chase wonders if as many people would come to his. Would people be devastated? Would some pretend to be devastated but go home and watch *Lost* and order a pizza?

Fuck Reed. He probably wouldn't even give a speech.

His phone jangles in his pocket, sending him into paroxysms as his nerves are unsheathed wires. It's a Connecticut number he doesn't know. But his intuition tells him that Laine is finally calling him. She's calling him now. When he can't put two words together. When he couldn't fake confidence with a sawed-off shotgun at his temple. So he lets it go to voice mail, and waits fruitlessly for a message. *At least she called me. She called me.*

He walks the strange streets of Charlottesville, passing bookshops and outdoor-sports-gear stores, groups of friends in fleeces and duck boots laughing and crowding the sidewalk. A vintage pickup truck goes by, the girl sitting next to the guy behind the wheel, his arm over her shoulders, a German shepherd with a green bandanna in the bed, letting the wind rush over his wild face, his hard nails clacking on the metal.

Nikki and Parker take the shuttle to town, and walk the extra mile to the sprawl outside Glendon. The parking lot is dreary, kids waiting in cold, rusty, dented cars while their parents shop. In the Laundromat, an obese man sits on two chairs and reads a newspaper. In the check cashing place, a man in a satin football jacket is arguing with the lady behind the glass.

"This is not your best idea ever, Nik," Parker says, hands deep in her raccoon coat, as they loiter outside the seedy liquor store.

"Listen, everyone else is in their own hometown or some shit for Long Winter Break, partying their ass off and having the best time. Boozing and smoking and whatever. We gotta at least give it a shot, no pun intended."

"I'm with you in that I wish we were having a good time, *however . . .*"

"Besides, we're off the radar here," Nikki assures her, wearing a black North Face jacket and white Chanel sunglasses.

"Riigghhtt," Parker says. "We really blend in."

"I'm just saying, no one gives a shit about the Green Book at old Wellington."

"They might care that we're sixteen. Remember the whole underage thing they have in this country? The whole you-have-to-be-twenty-one thing?"

"It's on me, Park. Chill. I know what I'm doing."

So they stand there in the cold, chins buried in jackets, hands shoved deep in their pockets. An old lady with hair sprouting from her ears and a housedress showing under her coat enters, and they let her. She comes out, the bells jangling again, with her paper bag. Moments later, a red-faced guy strides toward the store. Keys jingle from a belt loop. Nikki winks at Parker, and sidles up, blocking the guy from the door.

"Hey, there," she says smoothly.

The guy stops short, appraises her with untelling eyes that are opaque green.

Nikki tries her moves, pushes her glasses on her head, gives him a hangdog look, licks her lips. "Are you going in there?"

The man juts his chin toward the store. "In there?"

"Yeah."

Parker starts to step away, slowly, hopefully without anyone noticing.

"Why?" the man gruffly asks.

Nikki twists her body back and forth, hands in pockets, like a little girl. "'Cause I forgot my ID at home."

"And?"

Uh-oh, Parker thinks.

"I was just wondering," Nikki begins.

"You were just wondering," the man says, "if I was an off-duty police officer?"

Nikki is suddenly still.

"'Cause I am," the man says, imitating her baby voice.

Nikki now backs away, and then she and Parker slowly

walk backward. "You are?" she asks in a small voice.

The man reaches in his back pocket, probably for a badge, and the girls take off.

"Hey!" he shouts. "Hey!"

They don't even look to see if he's following. Nikki and Parker have never run so fast, so far, so hard. They run from the mall onto the service road, ducking the low branches of pine trees on the shoulder, skidding on icy patches, arms pumping.

"Oh shit," Nikki keeps saying.

They make it onto the main street of Glendon, duck down a residential lane. They heave, hands on knees, doubled over. Parker straightens up, hands on hips, looks down the quiet road and back at Nik. When she can finally catch her breath, she points out: "You shoulder-tapped a cop."

And this sends them into gales of laughter. They can't breathe. Parker hocks a loogie. "Jesus, I have to cut down on the cigs. I can barely run a half mile."

"Oh my *God*. That was retarded."

They link arms and walk, flushed, past houses with dark windows and white yards. Stone bird baths with ice in the depression. Christmas lights strung from gutters and unlit. They pass a teenaged townie couple, her hair dyed cherry-red and a ring through her nose, his baseball hat turned backward. They each have a hand in the other's back pocket. They don't glare at Nikki and Parker as the two pairs cross paths; they just flick their eyes up and away, pre-occupied with themselves.

"I have to tell you something," Parker says.

"You have a crush on Chase," Nikki says without pause.

Parker stands still and her jaw drops. "What!"

Nikki smiles smugly. "That's what you were going to say, isn't it?"

Parker laughs tightly, awkwardly. "Yeah. You're scary."

"Too bad he isn't here," Nikki says. "This is the perfect time to kick something off."

"He's in *Virginia*."

"Let me ask you something. Do you want it to happen?" They wait at a slushy intersection for the light to change. "Because you're so shy, he's never going to know, if you want something to happen I mean."

Parker and Nikki walk some more. "God, Nik. I can't say *anything* to him."

"It's so easy, girl."

"Maybe for you."

A pay phone is glistening in the winter sun, outside the pet store whose windows are empty. Nikki takes out her date book, slides a calling card from its inner pocket. "I have a number. I'll dial. You say hello, and what's up, Chase, and you tell him that you and I are hanging out and we felt like calling his ass because we're here alone and the campus is freaking *empty* and he needs to hurry back and save us and is he having a good time. See? Easy."

Parker's got butterflies fluttering up her throat. "It's not easy," she says, but has already let go, is already letting Nikki do this.

She takes the receiver while Nikki dials the number from her book. The black mouthpiece smells bitter, like rotted tobacco and animosity, and she swipes it with the cuff of her jacket. It starts to ring. Her heart pounds. Somewhere in Virginia, a phone is ringing.

"Hey, this is Chase, I'm not picking up my phone so leave a message."

She presses the silver hook, and giggles, high on the near miss.

Nikki slaps her arm. "You should have left a message!"

"I can't believe I just called him," Parker says, stunned by that alone.

Out of the wood shavings in the pet store window pops a puppy, his paws on the glass. He steams it up, clumsy tail wagging. The girls squeal and run to the tiny mutt with the pink belly.

9

After that *glorious* trip, coming back to Wellington feels like returning to the womb. Chase blandly responds to inquiries about his time at UVA—he talks beer, coy and willing girls, drugs, and games—and otherwise nestles into school life. Gets fetal in his room. Sucks down Welch's grape soda from the vending machine like it's breast milk.

Early March in New England is *not* springtime. The temperature occasionally reaches the fifties, but the quad is a soup of snow, mud, and dirt. Trees barren, sun rare. The Costa Rica trip is weeks off and the gang has finally solidified plans. Greg is out because of his cousin's wedding and Burns's parents want him in Rome.

The squash team plays Choate, and Gabriel creams Timmy Blanner, a distant Kennedy cousin, who throws the biggest sissy-fit anyone on the bleachers has ever seen. No one even laughs as he throws his racket against the glass, picks it up, and throws it again, because it's too weird. The fourth or fifth time he does this, cursing Gabriel out, the racquet ricochets back to hit Timmy's ankle, and then he hops all over the court, his face crimson and ugly.

Nutmeg experiments occur on Cadwallader 2. Ineffective except for Noah's delirium, which Noah eventually gives up. *It was wishful delirium,* he concedes. Like Beth Crandy and Toppy, who were given O'Doul's last spring by pranking friends and got so "drunk" Toppy passed out and Beth threw up.

Chase has officially left the idea of being good behind, as no one's gotten in any trouble and the threat that they will has worn thin. Chase has found a removable panel in his wall, and the guys all store their stash in there. Skoal, kind bud in vials, Parliaments. Burns even stores the pills he distributes sometimes, if he's feeling paranoid. The guys smoke weed, crouching in their own closets, blowing into balled-up socks. They fill water bottles with gin and lemonade, go for long walks in the woods, kicking at rotting trees, ripping leaves off vines.

There's just something about smoking a cigarette in a grove of melting snow with your buddy, standing under a paltry sun, one glove off to handle the cigarette, knuckles getting icy cramps as you talk, shuffling boots, saying—in a quiet and peaceful way—*screw you* to puritans everywhere in the world.

Misbehaving in general is a nice, cozy crawlspace away from the main room. It's a secret place, where authority can't find you. If you're high, you can stand a few feet from some anal teacher, but you can really be a million miles away, light-years from mundane existence. Safe from mediocrity.

Besides, Chase is sort of invincible. Swigging whiskey in a darkened room, the bottle being handed from silhouette to silhouette, Chase soars. His buzz is a genuine vibration of golden energy that forms around his body a kind of knight's armor.

Limnology lab is an unpredictably bright spot at the end of the week. He and Parker are assigned to the creek trickling under ice through Derrinder Grove. They carry jars into the deep misty shade, crouch in the dark cool. Chase collects the specimens, and Parker makes notes with her fingerless gloves, clutching a ballpoint pen and scribbling onto a notepad. Chase's nose is bright red at the tip.

The sun's been going in and out today, but when they emerge from the woods, it's out in full. They swipe snow from a big log and sit. Chase pulls out a napkin-wrapped sandwich from the dining hall. He offers half of the messy thing to her.

"What is it?" she asks.

"You probably won't like it. It's egg salad on pumpernickel, with red onion slices I pirated from the salad bar."

"Are you kidding? That sounds awesome."

They take off their mittens and eat under the early-afternoon sky, which is a hopeful and innocent shade of blue. The air almost hurts to breathe, it's so crisp, but it feels good, too. Chase can feel the exact outline of each lung when he inhales, the bitter air cutting the wall of his organ. They both point at the same time to a pair of deer, noses to snowy ground, who are strutting into brush across the fields. Parker and Chase chew, smile at each other wordlessly. Maybe everything will be okay, he thinks. Maybe everything is actually kind of excellent.

Later, he's sitting at his desk for study hall when his bowels jerk. Sweat breaks on his face so fast he wipes his forehead and then looks at a wet hand. His heart bumps. He's sick on his French homework, yellow puke flecked with purple onion bits, oozing over a sheet of conjugated *to be*'s.

Gabriel says something under his breath in Spanish. He looks aghast. Through his nausea, Chase absurdly thinks: *Now I know what that word means. "Aghast." It's the expression on Gabriel's face.*

Gabriel, unable to deal, must have notified Noah, who shows up in the stall where Chase is kneeling in his corduroys.

"Christ, you are *ill*," Noah says, surveying the trail.

"You think?" Chase says meanly, spitting.

"Easy, bro. Here, look at me."

Chase turns to his friend like a dying animal pleading with its master to put one between the eyes.

"Okay, we're going to the infirmary," Noah announces. "You look like a ghost, dude."

Chase is shivering, and Noah just grabs his own comforter instead of trying to fit Chase's trembling arms into a narrow coat. They make their way across twilit snow to the infirmary, plaid blanket dragging, their silhouettes strange to anyone looking from afar: a tall guy supporting the arm of what looks like a king in some royal cape.

The lights are low in the medical rooms, as the place is officially closed except for emergencies after six o'clock. Nurse Sinclair, in white, opens the door as they approach, as if she intuited that he was on his way. Her strawberry hair glistens against her uniform, her turquoise lash lines, the cheap tattoo under her white stockings. Chase looks at her, preparing to beg, since she's the sarcastic and belligerent keeper of the gate when it comes to days off and sick excuses. But he doesn't need to speak. She pulls him inside, rubbing his back with a meaty hand, and it feels good.

"All righty, guy. We're going to get you set up. You're sick, guy, I know it," she murmurs.

Chase is vaguely wondering how she knew, besides the

specks of puke in his long hair and his ivory gray pallor, and then he walks into the main room. There's Parker, legs above sheets, face pale and wet with fever, a bucket on the floor.

"Egg salad," Nurse Sinclair says. "Good old egg salad."

Chase runs to the bathroom, dropping the wet blanket, not sure which end of himself is the priority.

He lets the nurse lay her hand on his forehead, thermometer in his mouth, not sure how it got there. Not sure if the night is young or if morning is about to break, he's shirtless, sockless, but still in his cords. He sees his own pale ribcage shiver as if it were the ribcage of some other unlucky sucker. He loves the nurse. He wants to marry her. She's got that prison warden look, but he doesn't mind, it's totally cool. She gives him ice cubes to suck. She spoons him medicine. Coos words of kindness. *It will be over. It will.*

The curtains are drawn against stars or sun, and he closes his eyes again, hoping to vanish, to sleep, to go away. But the huge inner darkness becomes a globe, and the globe spins, and he's dizzy, and he's retching into the bedside bucket.

Darkness. Someone is trying to get him to change into a dress. Can this be? A white dress? It's the nurse. He pushes it away. He uses strength. Tilting darkness, a planet of dark, turning, twirling around another galactic body.

He opens his eyes. Nothing.

He opens his eyes. A girl sits on the edge of a bed, uneasy as if she's at a rich and aristocratic house. "Please, honestly, I don't want the applesauce today," she murmurs. She's wearing something pale lavender, and it ripples across the darkness.

Bang. He's awake. Light. White curtains billow and get sucked to the window, which is cracked to let out the air of sickness. No nurse in sight. Chase turns to see Parker, strewn across her own bed, her dark stringy hair twisting over the pillowcase. Milk-white arms clutching herself. The hollows under her eyes a gray violet. One leg above the sheets, in man's pants, bare feet. A lavender camisole.

Did he hallucinate Parker hallucinating last night?

Her brown eyes open. She stares, as if she doesn't know who he is. Then mortification takes over her features, one by one. "I bet I look really good right now," she croaks ruefully.

He smiles, looking like death himself. They turn away from each other to stare at the ceiling. Chase gets shivers, thinking that he hasn't slept in a room with a girl, not since second-grade sleepovers, and this has been a horrific way to start again. Suddenly he hears Parker cry.

"Parker," he soothes. "Are you okay?"

She doubles over and groans, because it must hurt. But she can't stop.

"Don't cry," he says, helpless.

This makes it worse. Suddenly she says, when she catches a breath: "Oh my God, Chase. I'm not crying, I'm laughing! We have the *worst* luck together; it's unreal."

Eventually he laughs too—chuckles at first, as he's scared of his stomach. Then he's overcome, and almost falls out of bed.

Nurse Sinclair wheels in meal trays. "Well, well, look who's feeling better," she smirks, but not unkindly.

When he can control himself, Chase asks her if she tried to get him to wear a dress. This sends Parker into gales of laughter.

"That was a dressing gown," Nurse Sinclair says in her working-class Connecticut accent, setting straws into water glasses. "Neither of you turkeys would change. You wanted to puke all over your nice clothes. This one"—she gestures at Parker—"has some kind of lacy underclothes on, for pete's sake."

Parker, hiccupping from laughing, smoothes the front of her pale violet camisole. "I was wearing it under my sweater."

"Hey, Park, did your mom by chance give you apple-sauce when you were sick, as a kid?" Chase asks.

"Yes. And how do you know that?" she answers.

"Ha! You were talking in your sleep last night. I thought I dreamed you dreaming but I didn't."

They both sit down and drink electrolyte drinks out of

plastic cups. *Cheers.* Neither had kept water down all night. Parker nibbles at bread. Chase looks at their surroundings. Ancient white iron beds match the tiled walls and curtains. Antique glass jars hold swabs and gloves. The infirmary is lost in time.

Parker must be thinking the same thing. "I feel like we're in some asylum in, like, 1945. Or we're kids dying of polio in some convent."

"Seriously," he says. "Where're the fucking leeches?"

"Jesus!" Parker says then, throwing the sheets off her. "First I'm freezing, then I'm hot."

"Yeah, me too," he says, peeking at her long legs. Lime-green polish on her toes, a gold anklet, the gold rubbed off the cheap metal on the dangling star charm.

"Uh-oh," she says after a moment. He feels it too. They race to the bathroom, wrestle to get in until Chase comes to his senses and lets the lady go first.

Guess it was too early for bread.

Lying in half light. It's interesting to see him like this, she thinks. All that dynamic golden-boy energy, all that sugar, leaked out of him. Those fast eyes and slow honey smile— all of it shut down. He rests quiet, his long hair greasy on the pillow, eyes half closed, his drawling and snarling mouth pale and quiet. *And Jesus, he's still beautiful.*

* * *

Nikki comes and goes, leaving a bag for Parker. Yellow sweatpants and a faded gray Johnny Bravo T-shirt. Library books from Parker's bedside table. Red apples. Toothpaste and tortoiseshell comb. A get-well note, with bubble heart and smiley faces.

In the blue afternoon, they disinterestedly page through the library books. A book of haiku with a Japanese character on the front. Chase reads through it, and then recites an ad lib poem of his own: "The room smells like ass. No guests for Parker and Chase. Egg salad no more." A biography of Jimi Hendrix. Books on Costa Rica, which should excite them but don't. An old guide to growing fruit trees.

"You, um, you planning on sowing an orchard on the football field or something, Park? Should I be concerned?"

She smiles as well as she can. "Don't know why I took that out. I just liked the quince blossoms and stuff. The idea of fruit trees, picking pears in the summer."

"Okay, there. I'm no further along in understanding why you checked this out, but thanks for at least trying to explain."

That's the majority of their weak conversation. They basically spend a few hours lying on their sides, facing each other, but silent. Mouths dry, bodies in limbo.

"You awake?" she rasps in the dark.

"Yeah."

He can't see her but he can feel her. She's there, the way a tree looms in the dark when you walk on a moonless night.

"How you feeling?" she asks.

"Eh. I've felt worse."

"I had scarlet fever when I was seven. I saw, like, these little angels, except they were kind of monkeys, and they tried to take me away."

He sees her words like bubble letters, floating through the dark room. "Are you serious?" he asks.

"Yeah, I mean it was fever dreams. But I wonder if it was also, you know, if I came close. Because my temperature spiked to a hundred and four degrees that night."

"My brother hit me in the head with a baseball bat, by accident. He was batting, and I got too close. I was out for a few minutes. And then I came to and he was standing above me, his hands bloody, this guy Will holding him back. He'd gone a little crazy when I wouldn't wake up and had been trying to wake me, trying to put my cut scalp back together. Like I was a toy or something. But he looked so relieved when I opened my eyes, Jesus. I'm sure it was just him hoping I was okay so he wouldn't get slaughtered by my mother, but who knows. It may be the one time I ever saw him give a shit about me."

"You guys don't get along?"

"I used to think we did, but, I don't know, lately it hasn't been good."

"That kinda sucks, Chase."

"Yeah, it kind of does."

"My brother's four years younger than me so he drives me nuts, but I adore him. He has the greatest little spirit. He panics a lot, he freaks out, but it's because he's got so much going on upstairs. He sleeps in my bed sometimes, because he needs to talk. Like if we'd seen some show where a lion killed a giraffe, he has to go through it point by point, in the dark, till he can let it go. *Yes, animals kill each other,* I tell him. *No, they don't hate each other. They eat each other; it's part of a food chain.* On and on."

"What's his name?"

"Finn. He's a cool cat. A little guy, really, but strong."

"You ever think about Mary?" Chase asks without any forewarning.

Parker's quiet for a second. "Whoa. Mary."

"You have any big theories on where she is? If she is? All that? Wow, I must sound like Finn."

Parker laughs. Then she's quiet. "I think about her all the time. I mean, *all the time.* Because when I'm not even thinking about her, my general thoughts have changed because of her. I'll never . . . I don't know. I'll never think that I have so much spare time again. But I don't know where she is."

"That's how I feel. It's like, I thought it was endless before. In the back of my mind, I thought we got a million chances," Chase says.

"We don't get a million chances."

They talk then, about how they were ashamed to be grateful to Mary for being the one. How they wondered what it would be like to vanish as she did. They admit they hoard the event, keeping the moment they saw the ski away from everyone who wants to take or share it.

As they talk, Chase realizes they're spilling pasts and presents and futures into each other's laps. Turn off the lights and they can say anything. Like someone unbuckled muzzles from their mouths.

They talk about "Home." Chase says he wishes he could have some sweet goddamn tea right now. Parker talks about a greenhouse her family once had, and how her dad grew tobacco and tea and medicinal herbs. They talk about choosing Wellington, and wondering if it's the right place.

Somehow they get onto the Gold and Silver Ball. Parker's describing her morning shame, even though she hadn't done much wrong. "It was like, you know, I put on my jacket—it was so cold that next day, remember?—and it's rabbit fur, and it had soaked up everything. Smoke, alcohol, grime, city air, the food from that deli we stopped in where they were frying something. And it was the worst feeling, wearing that thing. Like being wrapped in the worst part of the night."

"And the worst part was pretty bad," Chase says.

"It was. The worst part was pretty bad. . . ."

As she continues to talk, Chase thinks back to that night. He'd barely known she was there, he was so focused on Laine. He goes back to the beginning of the evening. There's Parker in a white dress with a shiny black ribbon around her waist. In Noah's kitchen with its track lighting and platinum appliances.

Long legs. All legs and arms, that girl, and dark hair that snaked down her back. Creamy skin. A mole on her chest, by her sternum. That stance, that way of standing in a group as if physically apologizing for being there. Her sloped shoulders meant she knew she didn't quite belong, but her uplifted chin said she would ride it out. And he hadn't done anything to make her feel differently. The cat eyes Nikki had done for her, making her look like an old-school movie star; had they met his own all evening? Or did they never even connect?

As their talk falters now in the dark infirmary, both of them stuttering into sleep, Chase relives the night. He goes so far as to *redo* it. He regreets her. Tells her she looks nice. No, he tells her she looks beautiful. He kisses her on the cheek. Before the night gets rough and dirty, he asks her to take a walk with him instead of going back to the hotel. They laugh, kick at litter on the cold street, arms linked in an old-fashioned way, her glittering bag hanging from her arm, and they have nowhere to go. They head that way.

10

Nurse Sinclair lets him use her big PC in the office. It's been two days so Chase anticipates an inbox of missed assignments and deadlines. He's groggy, not sure of the time and not caring. And then—*blinggg*—she appears on IM.

She says *hello* and *where have you been*. He explains how he and Parker ended up in the infirmary. She says she *misses him and thinks about him all the time*. He is vulnerable again. She says *feel better and say hey to Parker. Wrap a cold towel around your head*. She says *goodnight*.

Chase raises his heavy head to the stench of his emptied vomit bucket lying against the metal railings of the bed. His head lies in a damp spot. *Please tell me I didn't yack here.*

Chase sees a discarded towel on the floor. He remembers now that he'd wrapped a cold towel around his head, as Laine had urged him to do.

The nausea has passed, leaving him weak and craving the cheese toast and English tea his mother made on cold weekends in Charleston. His freckles have officially vanished, leaving him ashy and white as the infirmary walls.

It's still dark as he weaves to the restroom. He hears voices. He holds the bucket away from himself as he slides down the corridor in Patagonia socks. Christmas was lame this year; he complained so much about New England weather over Thanksgiving that his family outfitted him for a Nova Scotia trek.

Chase sees Nurse Sinclair through a crack in the door. Her pale pudgy fingers naked without latex gloves. An oversized winter coat over her starched uniform. She looked like the type of woman to be missing teeth. Which is not to say he hasn't grown to love her. She tells them about her poker games, play-by-play. She gives them town gossip, whose baby-daddy knocked up whose sister, whether the dry cleaners fire was insurance fraud. Parker and Chase meet her boyfriend, Larry, a big, Trinidadian guy who has somehow wound up in the whitest town in the United States. He sits in his Chevy, which trembles and shoots out exhaust, and she picks up her lunch from him, leans into the window to give him a kiss.

Chase pushes the door open, and sees Burns with Nurse Sinclair.

"Fuckin' egg salad, my man." He gives Chase a wink. "Got the runs like cuh-*razy*."

Nurse Sinclair hands Burns a plastic bag and a "Do Not Disturb" Red Card for his door. "Burns," Nurse Sinclair calls out as he's leaving. "No more days off this month, so enjoy it."

Burns glances at Chase, extends his palms, and shrugs as if to say: *I just have a gift.* Before he leaves, he suddenly doubles back to "tell Chase about French class." When he gets him into the room, Burns nods at Parker and chucks a few pills onto Chase's bed. "On the house, brother," he says.

Chase knows about Burns's connection with Sinclair. Burns has a casual practice with the student body; he orders pills from Canada or Mexico, sells them for eight times the price. Not that he needs the money. Maybe just the attention. Ritalin or Adderall for kids who need a leg up or want to rip a line Saturday night, and Vicodin and Xanax (and sometimes, the Holy Grail: Oxycodone) for hungover Sundays or the winter blues. Occasionally morning-after pills and Viagra. When he can't get, he heads to the infirmary with an envelope of cash. Nurse Sinclair skims off the tops of bona fide prescriptions called in for students; she's the archetypal bartender pocketing a percentage.

* * *

"Jesus, you've been out for a while," Parker says, reading in her bed. It's only afternoon but the winter light has been extinguished, and the windows are deep blue.

Chase yawns. "Yeah, I know. You feeling any better? You look better."

"I'm all right, but I heard they're keeping us here because they're afraid we have *E. coli* or something. I just want to go to sleep in my own bed. Although I've gotten so used to privacy down here."

Chase surfs channels. "Yeah, but it would have been pretty boring if we weren't here together. That's *too* much privacy."

Parker gives Chase a sideways look, then looks away. "No more *SportsCenter*, please."

"Fine, but if I don't get *SportsCenter* then no PBS or Discovery." He pats his bed. "Come sit with me, you can see better."

"Deal." Parker moves over to his bed, not looking at him, heart beating. "Throw on the news."

"Why? We'll get depressed."

Parker sighs and gives him a sad face. "We already are."

Chase flips to CNN and she pats him on the head, as if he was a good boy.

They lounge in his small bed, feeling hot and uncomfortable, but neither wanting to disturb the delicate and strange ecstasy of being this close.

Parker's fallen asleep on Chase's bed as Nurse Sinclair enters with Campbell's soup and crackers.

"Dinner ti–" Nurse Sinclair stops and catches Chase's eye. She mouths "sorry" and leaves the food on an empty bed.

"It's not what you think," Chase kids her.

"It better not be," she kids him back.

Chase hears JD talking to the night nurse in the next room. His accent reverberates through walls like a plucked bass string.

"Hey, bud," he whispers, tiptoeing in. "Just brought you a little something from Sulli's Garden, but I'll jet so I don't wake her."

Parker opens her eyes groggily.

"Hey. I'm so sorry to wake you." JD reaches out his hand. "I'm JD, by the way."

"It's okay." Parker's voice is hoarse. "Excuse me. I'm Parker."

She knows him; girls talk about him, even though he's a mystery to everyone. They think JD is handsome in a Lone Ranger way, a guy who rides into the sunset. He seems to have a big-brotherly thing for Chase, as though he's looking for someone to trust. Someone who will trust him. Desperation shines on his skin, like sweat. He's too pale, and that comes, Parker thinks, from something besides the weather. It's a sallowness generated from inside. Reminds her of her own father, when he's on the verge of being depressed.

"How you all feeling?" JD pats Chase's knee.

"We're getting there. Hopefully we can stretch this out to Friday. Then one week of exams and off to Costa."

Chase catches Parker looking at JD, and he's startled to see pity in her brown eyes. No one ever looks at JD like that. Chase turns back to JD, who suddenly seems run down to Chase.

"That's right," JD says, unaware of being observed. "You're going with your roommate, right?"

"Yep. Me, Gabe, Parker, Nikki, and Noah. Gabe's pop even threw in the private jet for us to roll in style from Hartford."

"Man, I'm jealous of you all." JD grins.

"What's your plan?" Parker asks.

"Nothing crazy. Miami, then maybe Palm Beach. A group of seniors."

"Should be fun, right?" Chase asks.

"Who knows, man? We'll make it fun enough. Do some fishing. Drink some 'roos."

"What you got for me, bud?" Chase taps the bag.

"I got you *both*—you selfish bastard—a couple orders of mac and cheese, and there's a couple sundaes that the nurse

142

put in the freezer for you."

Chase can't understand why JD got Parker food and then it hits him; Chase and JD had planned on watching the Duke/UNC game tonight before Chase got sick. JD simply kept his word but is now giving his food to Parker so she won't feel left out.

On JD's way out, while Parker's blowing her nose in the bathroom, JD pantomimes his approval of her with a shrug, indicating: *Why not?* And whispers: "She's a great girl."

Later, Chase looks at Parker asleep. Her body sprawled diagonally across her own bed, she hugs the covers to her pink cheeks, her eyelashes casting intricate shadows. He sees for the first time that her face is shaped exactly like a heart. She's almost too close to touch right now.

JD's right, he thinks. *She is a great fucking girl.*

11

What a bizarre few days. A piece of time folded and put in an envelope. Chase and Parker are so grateful to feel okay that they're reborn. Chase makes a show of blinking at the light, shielding his eyes as if in pain when they get close to the door, as if they've been kept underground.

He'd helped her with her coat as they left, her wrists white as iron straight from the fire, especially next to the graying cuffs of her canary-yellow sleeves.

Inside the coat, a name tag stuck to the label: *Samantha Eldridge.* One of her thrift-store garments. And right now Parker *does* seem like two people to him: the tall, bizarre girl he used to know, always on the periphery, who carried her Underwood typewriter into the woods on Sundays, who was gangly and aloof, who belonged to autumn, to last

Christmas, to preconceptions and archetypes; and then there's the new Parker, the one in the lavender camisole and men's slacks in a midnight room with white tile gleaming like teeth, the statuesque one, the eloquent one, the one walking with him now and making snowballs with her bare hands to chuck at Burns's window, the one who belongs to tomorrow, and to the next day, and to springtime and to Costa Rica.

"We're going to have such a good time," she says when he brings it up. "Can you imagine?"

The trip seems real to no one. A collage of preposterous ideas: surfboards, daquiris, howler monkeys, bathing suits, coconuts. Preposterous because none of that translates in the language of New England winter. And the planning has been two steps forward and one step back, with parents talking to each other at length, with money issues, chaperone requirements, passports, planes, permissions. Parker couldn't go and now can. Burns and Greg were coming and now they're not. It's been an evolving daydream.

Parker couldn't go and now can.

And even though Chase is ready, he still doesn't believe it's possible that the five of them will step off these icy grounds, get aboard an airplane, and land in Costa Rica. It's as if they've got itineraries to Atlantis, or the dark side of the moon, to Never Never Land.

Granted, it's still a manic time, full of all-nighters studying for midterms and writing papers, dirty Sundays throwing back cut-rate gin with Welch's grape soda chasers. Burns eats an entire tub of hummus and then shows Cadwallader how to light farts on fire—he actually scorches the bathroom wall. Greg and Chase get pizza in town one dark afternoon, and watch with the pizzeria owners out the window as an old VW van slides slowly, horn blaring, down the icy hill until it crashes into the front yard of a gray house at the foot. A white-haired, bearded old hippie, like a gnome, gets out and dances around, shaken but alive.

Squash is squash. The bench is the bench. JD and Chase take a cab all the way to Meyerstown for prime rib night at Lilliput's. JD throws down his card as always. *My dad says we need red meat to stay invincible, at whatever cost.* Parker and Chase collect specimens of winter stoneflies, write down facts and write up labs, get things wrong, get things right, pass dirty jokes on loose-leaf to each other, tell each other true stories while studying and think about editing the embarrassing parts out but include them anyway, make things up and then come clean and rescind, kick the sun and bask in the snow, walk in the woods and stay away from the lake.

One day, as they head out to do fieldwork, Parker says she has a treat for them. From her bag, with mittened hands, she pulls two cafeteria glasses she stole and a bottle of maple syrup. They pour syrup on snow and eat it.

"Yum yum!" Chase says. "Squirrel piss and acid rain."

"Oh, shut up. It's a natural snack." She laughs.

He makes her teach him to hand-roll cigarettes in one of the cabins. They shiver in the dank room. Under her fur hat, there's something wild and ancient about her face, like she could have lived in these woods two hundred years ago, raising wolves. She makes fun of his bare, chafed ankles.

"Sunshine boy needs some socks."

"Sunshine boy needs to do some laundry."

He sees again what he saw in the infirmary: that this girl has been here all along, with hair he could wind around his hand a hundred times. And she makes him settle into the present. Wherever she is at the moment is where she wants to be. It's more than that; she becomes the place. Parker is the cabin. With no glass in her windows, no shutters to close. Birds could fly through her.

They smoke, try to blow rings, sit quietly in the hideaway. The ice balls don't melt from their clothes. Parker exhales a perfect *O*. Beaming, she points to the wobbly thing. "Yeah. *That's* right."

"Well done, Cole. You're officially misspending your youth."

Pine needles jammed into the seams of the floor scent the space. It's time that seems simple and insignificant, time spent getting to the next thing, time spent waiting for life to begin.

12

The Glendon Taxi minivan navigates black ice as the sun comes over the frosted Berkshire Mountains. Old barns sit dangerously close to the slick country road, glistening with icicles.

The group in the minivan is discordant, their nerves scorched by midterms and no sleep. Their eyes bone-dry from staring at blue book pages and laptop screens, their consciousnesses ticker-taping with the date of the Kent State riots and the location of the island of Circes and the principle of Pascal's triangle. Warm, sweet air and tropical water is imminent, but no one believes it.

Chase is obsessing over a test question he missed: *Does a nymph have wings?* Of course *now* he recalls. A nymph is a juvenile, the step between a larva and an adult insect. It's in the form of an adult, but has no wings yet. *No wings. Shit.*

Chase and Gabriel sit in the back row of ragged, pleather seats, engraved with graffiti, and stare out the windows, the left one a smoky pane that looks like it was found in a junkyard and shoved into the frame. Glendon doesn't exactly run a fleet of chariots. Parker and Nikki share a Parliament up front and Noah rides shotgun next to the white-pompadour sourpuss they always get, whether for a dip run to Cumberland Farms or a trip to the Hartford airport. Though once fearful of her, they now affectionately call her Diane, or Dirty D for short. Her fondness for Marlboro Reds, her loose cab rules, and mum's-the-word policy endear her to students.

Noah puts on kids' sunglasses he bought from the variety mart in town; their lenses are rainbow, and in the shape of pineapples. He sticks out his tongue, and against the bleak Connecticut landscape, he's a portrait of anticipation.

"D, you got any Shakira?" Noah asks as he reaches to change the radio station. "This Journey marathon is killing me."

"You touch that dial, you die, son." Even Dirty D has her limits.

"Come on, D," Noah pleads. "We need some Costa Rican flava."

"Shakira is from Colombia, dumb-ass." Nikki exhales a

drag. "Settle down, for God's sake."

"Whatever." Noah turns to face the rest of the crew. "Speaking of, Nik, you going Brazilian this week?"

"Only if you shave your back, Sasquatch," Nikki shoots back.

Gabriel asks if they all remembered their passports. There's a round of nods, but Parker dives into the messenger bag at her feet.

"Oh, no." She rifles through her Trapper Keeper, which is plastered with stickers and glitter and doodles. "I know I put it in here."

"Eating more space cakes, Parker?" Noah says bitterly.

"Chill out, Noah," Chase says, looking anxiously into the folder.

"Shit." Parker groans, but as she examines her bag further, she finds it. "Sorry, I was being an idiot; it's right here."

"Yeah, you are an idiot," Noah says.

"It's NO big deal," Chase says, intervening.

"Easy, dude. I was joking."

Parker and Chase look at each other. They look away fast, because it's overwhelming and scary, the anticipation they feel.

The van finally reaches the Hartford, Connecticut, airport, where Gabriel instructs Dirty D to pull into the private plane marine terminal. Two men in pilot uniforms wait outside the entrance. They all get out onto the tarmac, as the gate clanks together again behind them, the van shuddering in the unimpeded, icy wind.

"There's Felix," Gabriel points at the stockier pilot. Chase leans over Gabriel to get a better look. "And that's Javier. They're great pilots, used to be military."

"Bad-ass," Noah says.

Dirty D says gruffly out her window: "Don't do anything I wouldn't do."

This stops everyone short, and they all stare at one another.

"Gross," Parker deadpans, and everyone cracks up. They follow the pilots through a gate marked "Authorized Access." Waiting on the runway is a plane like nothing they've ever seen. With a pear-shaped body and rear-facing propellers, it's straight from a Bond film.

"Sick! What kind of plane is that?" Noah asks, giddy as a kid who just unwrapped the toy of his dreams.

"It's a twin engine Piaggio Avant II," which Felix goes on to explain is known for its unique shape but even better known because the Ferrari family owns it. Gabriel mentions that his uncle has a thing for Ferraris.

"Cool." Nikki approves.

"It looks small. It holds enough gas?" Parker asks.

"We'll stop in Miami to refuel," Felix says. "Plus, we can't land in a bigger jet. Where we're going, the runway is too short. You'll see."

The cabin is big enough for nine people and as high-tech as the exterior. Noah and Chase begin fiddling with their new toy.

"Yo, check this out." Noah spins his leather seat 360 degrees.

"Whassup!" Chase finds a thirty-inch plasma TV hooked up to an Xbox 360. "Gabe, no wonder you kick my ass in Halo."

"I know, sorry," Gabriel says. He's always apologizing for things he did wrong, or right, for being rich, for being Colombian, for the fact that the catered lunch today is Nutella sandwiches because that's what he's always ordered on board.

"Do *not* be sorry." Chase looks at Gabriel. Chase wonders what it was like for Gabriel, growing up with private jets like most kids have SUVs. They've been living together the whole year but the difference between them is finally sinking in.

"Bingo!" Noah holds up a six-pack of Bacardi Superior airplane bottles from the minibar. "Will your uncle mind?"

"My uncle?" Gabriel laughs as he returns to his seat. "I doubt it. But go easy. He won't want us falling out of the plane when we get there, you know what I'm saying?"

The engine cranks up and the Piaggio rolls down the runway.

"Guess we don't get the old safety speech, huh?" Nikki

asks no one in particular.

"It's not like anyone listens anyway," Chase says.

"I do." Parker grips her armchair.

While they wait their turn behind a Delta 757, Noah holds up his glass: "This is going to be an epic Spring Break."

"It already is," Chase says and taps Noah's glass.

They reach altitude and coast. Parker reclines on a creamy leather couch. This thing is crazy: sinister as a wasp's body, exotic as a sex toy, black as Mickey Mouse's ears. The inside is perfumed with money and power, and she feels like she can sink into the rich air and fall into enchanted sleep. The drawers where soda and crackers are kept are gold-plated. The tables are tortoiseshell.

Everyone's let go of the frenzy of exploring and discovering and is now reading magazines, listening to iPods. Noah's calmed down, thank God, although his bad manners are completely innocent. Nikki's definitely starstruck; her spectrum of wealth is pretty short. It tops off at a second home in Westhampton and the newest Jaguar. Gabe is as comfortable as Parker's ever seen him, since this plane, in the middle of the sky, is closer to being his homeland than Connecticut is.

Even belted in, Parker feels like she might rise out of her seat, or maybe she's afraid of rising out of her body, into a dream.

And Chase keeps darting looks at her. He takes his ponytail out of the rubber band and then winds it back in. This is unknown territory for them both.

The flight to Miami is uneventful. They take off again, and then Felix tells the group to buckle up.

"Umm, aren't we, like, still over the middle of the ocean?" Nikki looks out her window to nothing but blue— blue sky, blue water, blue rocks, blue mists.

"The runway comes out of nowhere. We'll be fine," Gabriel says.

"Thanks, Gabe. Very reassuring," Parker deadpans.

"There it is." Gabriel points ahead. They all lean, straining to get the pilot's view. In the distance through lush trees—a tiny strip of concrete.

"Are those cows?" Chase points to cows roaming next to the runway.

Nikki crosses her chest and Parker squints. They bounce during landing and even Gabriel grips his seat tight. But they've made it. They have been profoundly transported. Chase is first off, greeted with hot, sweet, salty air mixed with the perfume of livestock shit. A tall man with a thick goatee approaches.

"Hola, Gabriel!" He lifts Gabriel in a bear hug. "Are these our guests?"

"Yes, Uncle Estéban. These are my friends from school."

"Ahhh yes, from the distinguished mental institution up north." Estéban smiles. His accent is strong and his English perfect.

Estéban's in white slacks, sandals, and a yellow linen shirt with the top three buttons undone. His newest hotel is being built a few miles from this town. He reminds Chase of an Argentinean soccer coach he saw once on ESPN during the World Cup. Estéban asks if anyone's been here before.

Chase says he's been bonefishing with his dad near Cancún.

Estéban laughs. "Cancún is not like here." He's a man of few words.

Two men load up the old Land Rovers, and the group gets going. Estéban zips around bouncing buses, past horses trudging through sun. The second Land Rover follows dangerously close, flying around the same obstacles to keep up. Chase, Noah, Parker, and Nikki are wide-eyed, looking at lush land strung with rusty razor-wire fences. The Rover hits a pothole and they're thrown so high, their heads hit the ceiling.

Flor Blanca's rooms are villas with platform beds, outdoor showers whose wood slats are overgrown with flowers, and terraces overlooking the Pacific. Everyone looks at one another mutely, unable to even joke around, as they get moved in to their spaces by the hotel staff. Finally, after

Parker and Nikki sit in dumbfounded silence for a while in their room, Nikki looks at Parker.

"Heaven," she says quietly.

Dinner at Estéban's villa is a feast of fresh tuna, fried plantains, and rice. The staff refills wineglasses without asking for ID. Flanking Estéban are two ladies dressed in ruffles and straps and lace, and Chase and Noah stare so blatantly that Estéban stares back to send them a message.

After dinner, the group heads to the hotel pool. They're as drunk on the tropical air as on the wine. Gabriel, Noah, and Nikki slide in, unabashed, in underwear, everyone too lazily intoxicated to change into bathing suits.

"So, you want to get in?" Chase asks Parker, standing near him on the edge. He's slightly off with her, not quite as cocky as usual. Normally, she'd be thrown in by now.

"I should go change."

"It's not like we didn't see each other practically naked in the infirmary. I'm going in." Chase strips down to blue Brooks Brothers boxers and dives in, leaving Parker standing poolside.

"Come on. Don't be chickenshit," Chase goads Parker when he comes up for air. "Get in!"

She looks at the crew, playing in the eerily lit pool. "I'm going to the real water, I've got to get in the ocean," she says, and walks off to the darkness.

* * *

They stand in the water. The hot, salty surf washes away some protective shell and their bodies can breathe.

He's skinny, she sees. His chest ribbed and indented like a rock, and he has red-brown nipples. His hair is dark at the tips where it's wet. And he's holding himself a different way, his arms out loose in the gesture of an embrace—but he isn't holding her. She lets her arms float the same way. Chase and Parker just stand close, arms out, as though they could or they will hold each other. His eyes half lidded, the rims wet in the moonlight, and his mouth shining. They stand and look at each other, pulled apart and held together by some elementary force.

The next morning, Chase lies between dream and reality. Blue light oozes under the half-drawn shade. And then he remembers the night.

Swimming. Their clothes like trash washed up on the shore, clumps in the dark. Running their hands hard over the surface to splash each other.

The momentary limbs, the fragments of fingers and hands and faces, the sleek hair in starlight. Similar to his fantasies, swimming had been a torture of glimpses, of knowing what was there but not seeing it, of brushing flesh underwater but was it thigh or rib or arm?

He and Parker had talked casually as if they'd been standing on a city street corner catching up, but instead they were languishing in water. Parker's cheekbones glistened, hair conforming wetly to her neck until it floated around her shoulders. A wild, wild sky.

Oh no, he thinks, clutching his sheets like a baby blanket. *We didn't kiss, did we? Tell me we didn't.*

He remembers now that they'd come to the shallows, Parker using her forearms to pull herself forward on the sandy bottom while staying hidden under the dark green. And then she directed him with her chin, told him to get out first. They argued, and he sighed, giving in. Asked her to close her eyes. She giggled like a dirty old man.

He'd dressed and was turned away, staring disconsolately at a banana tree so she could get out—but he couldn't resist turning to look. He was reminded, right before he did, of that myth from Foster's Greek Lit 203, where Persephone is let out of Hades forever if she can walk to the exit without turning back once. She fails. And is doomed to spend a portion of her days underground.

Parker was hopping on the beach, one ankle in denim cutoffs, long hair fallen down, white body glimmering. Chase smiled. *I see a beautiful girl, head to toe.*

Between her legs in that one moment, a dark glint. Parker must not wear underwear.

The footage grinds to a sandy halt, as though he's looking at naked pictures of his sister. His mind is a dog, and he trains it away from Parker, knocks it on the nose with a rolled-up newspaper, and the dog whimpers.

"Screw me," he groans, wondering what she'll expect from him now. "Oh, *Christ*." He groans louder, as he remembers that although they didn't kiss, they *held hands* on their walk back to the rooms. Why is it so easy to want one thing at night and then not want it anymore in a matter of hours?

The boys parade barefoot down the sun-baked boardwalk to the café, sad creatures bloated from travel, pale from winter.

"You guys ever had a *bedida*?" Gabriel asks, eyes small above travel-puffy cheeks, as he scans the menu. "You gotta try a mango bedida. So good."

"Yeah, and I want what that guy over there is having," Noah says, squinting at a plate of papaya. "That looks awesome. And pineapple pancakes, dude."

But Chase isn't looking at his menu. Along the path he can see two pale bodies approach, wrapped in sarongs, the two girls' heads tilted toward each other as they walk. Girl talk. Gossip about last night swarms like bees around their heads.

Before Nikki and Parker close in, Chase nonchalantly introduces the idea of a guys' day today.

"You think they'll mind?" Gabriel asks.

"Nah," Chase says, waving his hand like Gabriel was

crazy. "Girls like to hang by the pool, drink piña coladas, talk shit all day. They don't *want* us around."

The girls swing tote bags as they approach.

"So what's the plan today, you guys?" Nikki asks, as Parker hovers in the shade, trying not to look at Chase.

"Well, we know what we're doing. You ladies are on your own. We're having a guy day. ATVs and the surf break up north a bit," Noah says.

Nikki and Parker exchange a look. "Why?" Nikki asks.

"Chase proposed guy plans and that's the way it goes, girls. Don't cry," Noah says.

Chase sees Parker's face fall. She immediately puts her features back together, with precision and effort.

Noah, Chase, and Gabriel take four-wheelers up the road, raising dust past candy-colored houses. Chickens strut in the heat. Flowers Chase has never seen before yawn off their vines, entwined around rusting fences.

They drive onto a virgin beach like cowboys. They unknot the cords securing boards to bikes and step into the broth, ankles leashed, fingertips guiding the fiberglass planks as they look into the white crash.

"Christ," Chase mutters, as he feels the pull and rage of stronger water than he's ever known. *Noah's going to kick my ass,* he thinks, since Noah constantly brags about his surfing prowess.

He shouldn't have worried. Chase is the only one who can catch a wave and stand.

"You suck, Noah! You're so full of shit," Chase catcalls as Noah flicks his wet hair from his eyes again, rising after one more rinse cycle.

"Screw you," Noah says scornfully. "The sun's in my eyes. I need a visor, you turd."

"Turd?" Gabriel asks, his accent making the statement funnier.

They spend hours paddling, catching, gliding, falling, rising. Chase forgets that there's anything in the world besides blue. The guys have no thoughts; they just exist.

In the shade, they collapse on the sand, lying without towels, looking up into the leaves and white flowers of an almond tree. The slightest breeze moves the leaf-shaped shadows on their bodies. They smoke cigarettes without talking. Chase doesn't think once about Parker.

Parker and Nikki take late-afternoon naps in the clean hotel sheets. Parker feels woozy, sick from too much sun. One showers and then the other, rubbing their skin with the big towels, trying to gain some equilibrium in the strange room.

"He's being a dick," Nikki starts.

But Parker holds up her hand to stop her friend. "Nik. I just don't want to talk about it."

When she's brushing her teeth, Parker knocks the water

glass from the sink. It breaks on the tile floor. Nikki helps her pick up the pieces.

* * *

When they get to the hotel bar, Nik and Parker are sipping red cocktails in the lavender twilight. Dresses pleated where they'd been folded into suitcases, hair wet, skin creamy with lotion.

"Hey, y'all," Chase says as energetically as he can.

Noah can't even make words, nor raise his hand very high in greeting.

"Did you guys have fun? Are you starving?"

The boys nod weakly. They try to drink and keep up with the girls, but eventually Gabriel clears his throat.

"Dude, I'm sorry, I think I've got to crash."

"Oh my God, so do I," Noah says.

Chase shakes his head in apology. "Me too."

Their muscles have started to burn. And their skin is feverish from being in the sun. The boys slide their aching bodies into beds at eight o'clock, while the girls shake their heads.

"Okay, seriously," Nikki says to Parker, as they share a dish of quickly melting mint ice cream.

Parker keeps her head down, and the big rubber plant leaves hush and shush in the breeze. Strong men with dark skin and New Zealand accents do shots at the bar. On the wooden ceiling, a gecko has managed to get half a moth into its throat, and the other wing sticks out of its small beak like a handkerchief. *I'm too embarrassed,* Parker thinks.

"You shouldn't be embarrassed," Nikki says, reading her mind the way that she does.

"Well, it's embarrassing, though."

"No, it's just the way it goes in the beginning. People are afraid of each other, so you take one step to the other person and then two steps away."

"Well, the little problem is that I don't do that."

"But you should. And you can," Nikki proposes.

Chase sleeps for fourteen hours. When he wakes, it's the same day as yesterday: turquoise and gold, the air bubbling like champagne with heat, the hotel stirring.

As the guys amble down the boardwalk, they see two surfers getting a Rhodesian ridgeback to leap for a stick of driftwood—for the benefit of two girls under white umbrellas.

"We got girls at twelve o'clock," Chase says.

Noah's squinting too. "That's Parker and Nikki."

"No, it's not," Chase says.

Gabriel laughs. "Yeah, man. I'd recognize Nikki's melons from a mile away. Put your glasses on."

Chase watches them out of the corner of his eye as the boys drink guava juice and watch a 1976 Brazilian surf video on the bar TV. When Noah asks if they should hit their spot again, Chase acts like Noah's being impolite.

"Nah, we need to hang with the girls today. It would be messed up to bail two days in a row, Noah."

"Easy. You were the one who suggested it."

"Yeah, I suggested it *yesterday*."

When Chase wanders down to Parker and Nikki, the girls are packing magazines and sunglasses into bags. "We're going up the hill to have lunch at this guy's house," Parker says. "It's like an eco-house and stuff; we're going to check it out."

"Not those guys that were just here?" Chase says.

Parker nods.

"How *old* are they?" he asks, flustered.

Parker and Nikki stifle laughs. Nikki pats his chest. "Oh, Dad, we'll be back before midnight, 'kay?"

Nikki and Parker take an ATV up the hill, and dust rises around them. Nikki drives, Parker holding her waist. The machine is loud. Howler monkeys, a baby on the mother's back, gaze from the trees. Burning trash smokes along the roadside.

"Do you think this is the right thing?" Parker shouts into Nikki's ear.

"Hell, yes! Fight fire with fire, babe. He's just scared, and the best medicine for fear of getting what you want is fear of *not* getting what you want."

Parker leans her head back, lets her hair trail in the wind. It feels good, and she smiles at the tropical sky.

The house looms in its yard, the gate unlatched. It's made of driftwood, and it's wide-open: just a floor, and a plastic roof covered in dried palm branches. No walls, no doors. Candles and bouquets of flowers in every niche. Incense smokes, suffusing the air with sandalwood.

A redheaded woman with yellow eyes and a zebra-print sarong knotted into a dress offers them a drink. She holds up a pitcher: "I soaked zee mango in cognac zrough zee night, then pour on zee vite vine. Very zimple, dahling."

Dogs and cats slide like shadows under bamboo tables, and people sleeping in the hammocks strung between trees rise up like ghosts. Tiki torches flame in the daylight.

A white-haired Tico with mahogany skin asks where they're from.

"Well, we go to school together. At Wellington," Nikki says.

"We're from the United States," Parker amends, being the better-traveled one, the one who knows that "Wellington" doesn't ring any bells here.

"Ah," the gentleman says.

Parker becomes fixated on a baby walking with barely mastered steps. His mom and dad are deep in conversation but have an eye on the child, not needing to break their talk to guide him away from candles or keep him from waking a sleeping mastiff. She hears the father, who's young, strong, and wild-eyed, explain that he's from Barcelona and his wife is Finnish, and they live here now but might move to Panama in a month.

The child's face is half lit and golden, and he sits down to play with a yellow coconut, banging it on the stone floor. His mother's Thai silk skirt is close enough for him to touch, and he does so just because he seems to catch the emerald and turquoise shimmer. Then he goes back to rubbing the hard fruit. Parker wonders if the kid will remember this house with no walls, or if it will go unremembered but still factor into his soul. *Who are you going to be?* she thinks, looking at the blond head.

This is one of those places where it's impossible to tell who's American or who's international until they speak. Countries cross-pollinate as groups drink and surf and fall in love. People sleep in tents on other people's land. They eat mangoes from the trees. Parker loves this house, how birds and butterflies fly through it. She feels her own person losing its walls, her self bleeding into the land like the incense smoking through the rooms and out to the ocean.

The girls come back after sunset, Nikki wearing beads someone made and Parker in an orange cowboy hat. They're yawning but bursting with stories. The surf cooperative was ringed by guava trees, a beehive murmuring in the yard.

Sweet-tempered pit bulls sought out shadows in the house. They'd made ceviche from fish caught that morning, squeezing limes with the other guests around a stone table.

Gabriel suggests dinner, and the girls say sure, they'll come, but they've been eating all day. They'll just have drinks.

The next morning, Chase gets up early. The light is creamy, and he wanders the hotel.

He finds Parker in the lobby, her head bowed over a book, papaya on a fork, not yet eaten but not put down, forgotten. A strand of hair hanging, the rest braided. A diaphanous white tunic.

"Good morning," he says, formal and awkward. "Can I pull up a chair?"

She looks up. "Of course."

"How did you sleep?" he asks, as if they were strangers.

"Good. Good, and you?"

"Fine, thanks." He looks around. Fiddles with his napkin. "Listen, why don't we go for a walk, before the beach gets too hot?" she says.

He looks in amazement. She's never suggested anything before. He gets up to go, smiling. It takes Parker at least ten minutes to get over it herself, the fact that she spoke up, and that she asked for something that she wanted, and that she got it.

They walk a couple miles, dragging their feet through the surf sometimes, picking up shells to look at, pointing out sunrise surfers, silhouettes of tanned shoulders bobbing in waves.

They could be in any Eden. Where the shells are whole, unbroken. Where dogs wait at the edge of the water, watching their owners surf. Chase and Parker talk. About Gabriel's uncle. Their hotel rooms. The plane ride. Nikki's salon tanning before they left school. Noah's obsession with partying here, so he'll have a story for Burns.

And they spend stretches in that silence they've experienced before, looking at lush jungle that meets the sand, houses tucked into green palms. Balinese homes, and concrete tropical bunkers. Iguanas bathing in the heat on rocks, their lizard eyes derelict and ecstatic.

"I'm just so glad we're here," Parker says. "What if we weren't?"

"I love your logic, Park."

13

They all burn, even with sunscreen. They get red marks on spots they forgot: the back of the calf, a triangle by the bikini halter strap. But long days in the sun even everything out. They all get comfortable in fewer clothes. Nikki gives up heels. Parker gives up shoes. No one combs their hair. Chase lives in old-school white OP cord shorts, no shirt, his long hair tangled into a ponytail. Tip of nose pink, skin brown.

"I could live here," Noah says one day, sipping a banana bedida by the pool.

Gabriel's in the pool, sipping his own bedida. "Let's not go back."

They do yoga in a Japanese teahouse on the hill. The sanded-wood room is open on four sides, and high enough to see the coast. Tiny figures down there in the water are surfers catching the sunset ride. Noah, the least flexible, attempts downward dog, having fallen head-literally-over-heels in love with the Argentinean instructor, Carmen.

Chase has been to Mexico with his father, brother, and a bunch of other guys. The only local men they got to know were guys cutting their fish on the docks. They drank what they drank at home—Johnnie Walker, Belvedere, Coors Light—and called their wives at a set time each evening from plush and air-conditioned hotel rooms. They kept their own world intact around them like a life preserver. But Mal Pais dissolves Chase's idea of his own life. It's changing him.

The crew walks differently. They let hands linger on one another's shoulders. It's affection let loose from winter bindings. They talk differently. Spend time over coffee, taking the time and risk to tell stories about their families, childhoods. They throw scraps of fried plantains to the iguanas, who catch the food with a primeval snap of jaw. They collect fallen jasmine flowers, petals browning, smell the divine center. In the hottest hours, they retreat to their rooms, lie in bathing suits on their beds and read books. At night, they walk to the ice cream shop, lick their cones as they slowly make their way back to the hotel.

Chase teaches Parker to surf in the whitewater. At first she's concerned with her body and how the bathing suit covers it and what Chase can see this close up but that all passes quickly. She falls again and again. She finally learns how to catch the end of the wave, jump up on the board, and ride before letting herself land sideways, into the froth.

"Oh my God, this is so hard!" she says, coming up, shaking water from her face.

"You're doing awesome," Chase tells her honestly. "Standing up is the primary part. If you can do that, you can surf, Park."

They hike the nature preserve. The woods are fragrant and green. As they round a giant tree split by lightning or disease, they see thirty or forty tiny bats perched in its trunk. Like little black dumplings, hanging from meticulously small feet. At the end of the trail, pelicans thrive in the cove, flying down the thin, transparent curls of big waves to see fish—occasionally reaching a talon in to snag a flapping, silver body.

Chase and Parker have an unspoken arrangement. They always walk side by side. Inside the group, they are their own group. Whenever everyone's talking, Chase catches her eye, and they have an additional understanding.

Chase and Parker are eating fish burritos at Palma Royale, and talking to the guys from Bellingham, Washington, next to them. They'd worked nights and weekends during their last school year, and then all this past summer, to save for traveling Central and South America. They've seen Nicaragua, Panama, Chile, Argentina, and Mexico. Finding their way. They worked two months building homes in Nicaragua for Habitat for Humanity, and after Costa Rica they're headed to a permaculture farm in Ecuador.

"Are you going to college in September?" Chase asks.

"Not sure it's the right thing, now," one of them says. "Might work with my dad in plumbing; he's union, he can get me in. I just don't feel like borrowing as much as I need for college."

The two look scratched, bruised, used, burned, and radiant. They're public-high-school educated, and without plans or means for further education. Chase stares, trying to register how many things they know that he doesn't.

"Don't idealize it," Parker warns him later.

"I don't need to, it's cool as it is," he protests.

"It's *not* when they get stuck in lives of manual labor, punching a clock, to make up for this year of travel."

"You think the rest of their lives will suck? Come on."

"I'm not saying that. I'm just saying don't be jealous. They *work*. You don't know that part of the equation."

"What, are you some kind of farmhand when you're home?" Chase jokes.

She looks at him. "Yes. Kind of."

"But you haven't, like, *worked* worked."

She sips her orange Fanta and laughs at him. "Yes, I have."

That night, Parker sees a small blossom of brightness down the beach and she pulls Chase from the bar. The trip is over in a couple days, and she's instinctively pulling him away from everyone whenever she can.

The fire dancers draw symbols on the night by swinging kerosene-soaked rags tied to blackened chains. One girl lets Parker try. She whips the burning ball above her head in a circle, her face painted with light along its exhilarated bones.

They watch for a while, then start to head back. He walks behind her, as she's energized by the fire, and she's making those long strides on the wet, lustrous beach. The sleeves of her red Mexican dress bare her shoulders, golden and prominent.

"God, that was so medieval," she says, sniffing her hands. "I smell like gasoline. That would never be legal in the States."

"Yeah," he says, distracted.

"You should have tried it, why didn't you? Hello, Chase, you there?"

He keeps forgetting to answer her because all he can think of doing is saying: *Park, wait a sec.* And he'll put his hands on her arms and kiss her bewildered mouth. He can see it. *Park, wait a sec.* He holds her. He kisses her. *Wait a sec.* He does this over and over, but meanwhile his legs keep marching, hands stay in pockets. He nods at her, and then the hotel lights are smoldering there in the dark jungle, and the chance is past, and they turn into the beachfront gate. *What am I afraid of?*

Estéban never becomes less intimidating, but his chaperoning technique is hands-off. He'd talked to Gabriel before the trip about drinking, and Gabriel had asked the group to at least keep it in check.

"My uncle is cool, right? But no fucking up your rooms and stuff. Okay?" Gabriel had been nervous to ask.

And of course Noah pushes it most nights. One night, they try guaro, and Chase sees stars as he goes to sleep. Noah pukes on two nights, and cited food poisoning in the morning.

"Whatever," Gabriel said, fed up.

But this is their last night. Tabu's DJ plays reggaeton that thunders under shooting stars, and its beach rages with four bonfires. They stand and drink Imperials around the flames, their faces gold, their hopes high.

"Let's get some blow," Noah says too loudly, his eyes already at half-mast. "Everyone and their mother is obviously high here."

"Why don't you say that louder?" Nikki says.

"If I get it, will you guys do it?" Noah asks, not listening to Nikki.

They all look at one another, wanting and not wanting to do it. Parker looks longest at Nikki. She wants this to be an incredible night, and coke is going to get in the way.

"I don't know," Nikki says.

"Fuck it," Noah says. "I'm getting it."

As he stalks off, Chase runs after him. "Wait up, man. Let me help you out."

They stand in the parking lot, a sandy grove of motorcycles and ancient Land Cruisers. They don't meet anyone there, so they roam the dirt road, looking meaningfully at passersby, communicating that they want something. They finally end up in the back of a white brokedown pickup, driving—engine roaring with effort—up a hill to a house where the driver claims they can buy.

"This is beginning to freak me the fuck out," Chase says, as the vehicle heaves in the pitch-black, and he's thrown against Noah.

"Come on, it's totally cool," Noah says with cobbled-together ease.

And then they get to the house, and Noah is silent. Two rottweilers sit at attention outside a grubby door. A chain-link fence rusts. Mexican rap shakes the woods.

"I'm not going in there," Chase says quietly.

Noah is staring at the window, chewing his lip, where

the silhouette of a girl is moving to the beat. She turns to them. They can't see her features exactly but a gold tooth glints.

The driver and his friend don't even talk to the boys. They smoke in the cab. Noah gets up unsteadily in the truck bed, steps over the side. Chase grabs his arm. "This is retarded, Noah. Come on, let's just get out of here."

Noah shakes him free and gives him a dark look. Chase doesn't go in with him.

Five minutes. The music goes off. Chase feels like pissing his pants. *Why am I here? Why am I not with Parker, sitting side by side on the beach, alone, talking and throwing stones at the surf line?*

The music is changed, now it's fast salsa, which sounds derelict in the situation. Ten minutes. *What am I actually afraid of?* Smoke curls from the truck window. Chase is picturing bad things. And he wants to be back at Tabu. He stands in the bed, he knows he should go in there, but he can't make himself move. Fifteen minutes. Chase is walking to the door. Knees buckling. Suddenly Noah comes out, ashen, triumphant.

"Let's go, fuck the truck," Noah says, patting his pocket.

They run in the absolute darkness, stumbling into the unknown. Noah does fall, sucks the ham of his hand, but they keep running. At some point they start laughing, shrieking in the Costa Rican night, alive and scared and free.

The bathroom lines are long at Tabu, so they all decide to go back to the hotel room. Parker keeps trying to get Chase's attention, but he's almost avoiding her. They sit on the beds in the guys' room, watching Noah cut lines with his bloody hand. Chase looks at Parker, in her white dress, red coral around her neck. Sand on her feet. She meets his eye. He finally meets her eye, silently asks if she's sure she wants to do this. She shrugs halfheartedly.

"Okay, my friends," Noah says, holding out the framed picture of an orchid, five fat lines on the glass. "Giddyup."

Nikki waits with the treasure while Noah rolls a hot-pink bill, with its leopard and Spanish letters, into a straw. As he's handing it to her with pomp and circumstance, though, someone raps on the door. Chase is simultaneously scared and relieved.

"Holy, holy shit," Gabriel whispers urgently.

"Oh my God!" Nikki whispers hoarsely, panicking. "What do I do with this?"

"Get in the bathroom," Noah says. "Go!"

Chase looks at Noah. "Get rid of it, dude," he says more calmly than he feels. "Dump it all."

Noah hands her the two bags. He shoots daggers at Chase. Parker goes with Nikki and they flush the goods, scrambling over each other.

Estéban's ivory silk shirt ruffles slightly in the breeze. "We leave at eight tomorrow morning. Is everyone ready?"

Clothes and toiletries are spread throughout the room. They look at each other, too nervous to think straight.

Chase steps up. "No, sir, we're not ready."

Estéban laughs as he turns away. "Well, be ready."

They open the minibar and do shots of Flor de Caña, the syrupy Nicaraguan rum. While Parker is peeing, Nikki nudges Chase and whispers: "What are you so afraid of?"

What a good question. I've been asking myself the same thing.

As Parker comes out, Chase stands up, with effort, the rum having set fire to his spine. He offers to walk Parker to her room. No one laughs, but everyone wants to— amused by his suddenness and courtliness. Parker accepts, blushing.

They know they aren't going to her room, and walk to the beach. At the horizon, a pale line. The suggestion of a new day. They sit on the sand, which has cooled. They don't talk. Parker rains palmfuls of sand on her feet, until Chase turns her head with his hand. He looks into her eyes, wet and wide in the moonlight, and he kisses her lips. The simplest, easiest, truest kiss of his life. They lie back. They kiss again, and she pulls his chest to hers. They are quiet, almost motionless, for what seems like hours, lips together, warm and shivering torsos together. Rum and rose balm on Parker's mouth. They don't do anything else. They don't take off their clothes.

And Chase is overcome. For everything he ever dreamed, he didn't know to dream of this.

On a couple hours' sleep, the group is grumpy, sad. They separate at the San José airport this time, since they're flying to their own homes. Chase and Parker sit in the waiting area, eating candy bars and trying to read magazines. Parker's eyes are red. Chase misses her and they haven't parted yet.

Her flight is called. She hugs everyone, kissing Gabriel on the cheek, thanking him. She laughs at something Nikki whispers in her ear.

Chase holds one of her hands as she shifts her bag on her shoulder. "Shit," he says ruefully.

She laughs. "This sucks. Why don't you just come with me? I'm sure your parents wouldn't mind," she jokes.

"Seriously."

Chase feels homesick except not for home. For the piece of time that just passed.

"You're amazing," Chase says into her neck as they hold each other. Then he holds her at arm's length. "I'm kind of amazing too," he says, cracking a grin.

She play-slaps him, smiling through glassy eyes. He pulls her back and kisses her and then watches her walk down the hall to where the plane's door is open like a mouth.

One by one they leave Costa Rica, headed for Canada, Colombia, South Carolina, New York. Two weeks of Spring Break remain. When Chase steps into Charleston air that night, Mal Pais will be lost. Cove by sapphire cove. Mango by mango. Wild dog by wild dog. Day by day and night by night, sunrise by sunset, the experience will fall away from him. He'll get pale, and forget being barefoot. His posture will get formal. He'll tell stories of the trip until they become stylized.

But he won't forget lying with Parker Cole on a beach turning pink at dawn. He won't forget her standing to stretch, brushing sand from her knees, a blush of sun streaming through her white dress. The water catching blue fire with a sudden day behind her.

14

Parker and Blue peel potatoes at her house, while her mom dices celery. Bluegrass on the university station. Her mom never preaches, but doesn't hold back ideas from them, either, and they've been talking about the rise of girl martyrs in the Middle East, which she's studying.

"God," Genevieve says. "Everyone just wanted to be a cheerleader when I was growing up. Replace that with dreams of dying in a ball of chemical fire, and taking others with you."

Blue looks at her, his eyes rimmed in kohl. A dirty potato peel on his skull ring. "Whatever that space is in between, that's where most teenagers live, I think. And I'm probably closer to the Armageddon side of things."

"Yes, Blue, I think you are," Parker says, laughing.

Genevieve doesn't tell him he'll grow out of it, or that he shouldn't talk, as he knows nothing of what it means to be a kid in Lebanon. She knows he knows things. He's been bossed around in enough homes and told what to think by too many mothers who were not really his mother. She doesn't pity him, though, or baby him. She loves him, and better yet—she likes him.

"FYI," Blue adds. "I'm not blowing up Tamkins High tomorrow; that's not what I'm implying, guys."

"So glad to hear that," Genevieve answers, stirring the beef stock, the black-maroon broth that perfumes the kitchen.

"I think my new teenage dream is to break into the old Royal rink, do some stoned roller-skating in silence. That place on Highway 8 is so freaky. I love it."

"So you've given up the immortality goal, now you just want to roller-skate?" Parker asks, simulating disappointment, knocking her peeler against the rim of the sink.

"What about the vampire plan?" Genevieve asks.

Blue smiles and shrugs. Then he turns to Parker. "What's your dream, sister?"

Parker smiles, suddenly shy. Finn gets up from where he was lolling with Raisin the cat, yawns. He's standing under the skylight their father made, a square hole in the roof to let in the stars. He announces that he's hungry.

"I have to keep it to myself or else it won't come true," Parker says.

"That's for birthday candle wishes only," Blue says.

"Whatever," Parker says, getting apple juice from the fridge.

She's going back to school tomorrow. She's going back to where he is.

At 10,000 feet the captain announces that flight 193 from LaGuardia will be making its descent into Hartford. At roughly 7,000 feet Chase sees that what he thought were clouds is snow. *You've got to be kidding. Snow on March 26.*

He looks out at the sky now and thinks about the final weeks of Spring Break, which passed like kidney stones. He surfed at Folly Beach, but the water was cold, the sets small. When his midterm grades arrived, his old man sloshed a glass of bourbon in his fist as he yelled. "This isn't good enough. Period, amen."

"What if it's good enough for me?"

"You're not listening, son," Randall drawled with menace. "*I* say what's good enough."

Chase hung his head and slunk to his bedroom.

Charleston in March is a velvet drug; cows stumbled in fields, birds flew sideways. Buds everywhere, hard as stone. In the bay windows of Battery mansions, forsythia was forced, blazing out of Chinese vases. Gray seas pounded the city, telling it to hurry.

Chase and his dad went fly fishing. This was Reed's

thing, but he was in the Dominican Republic with his frat brothers. Chase handed his dad the wrong fly.

"Does that *look* like a Swivel Face August Greenfly? Think, son, *think*."

But Chase hooked a trout. They stunned the fish on the head with the wood bat, and its milky rainbow scales coated his hands, and his hands shimmered too in the shade of the river trees.

His father was jubilant: "Jesus Lawd, *look* at that thing," he said over and over.

Chase wished to hell his moods didn't rely on Randall Dobbs's moods, but nothing ever made him happy like making his dad happy.

A party was thrown at the yacht club for his parents' twenty-fifth anniversary. Chase ripped through champagne. In the dining room, there stood an old photo of Randall, struck by puppy love, courting Vivien in someone's garden, her young mouth redder than the dusty pink dogwood flowers spangling the tree. Chase wasn't paying attention to his dad's toast—he heard him say something about Vivien being better than himself—until there was silence, and Chase looked up from the pill-balls of dough he was making from bread. Randall Dobbs raised his glass with a trembling fist because he couldn't finish. The room was hushed. Vivien held his forearm with delicate fingers.

Chase gaped—mystified, terrified, mesmerized.

He shot Natural Light cans off the bulkhead with Luke, took bong hits in Spenser's barn, the stench of hay not unlike marijuana. He ate grilled cheese and tomato soup at home, feeling low after being high all day, watching ESPN as rain came down. Before he left for school, he knocked back a quarter bottle of his dad's special bourbon, leaving a message in the Morse code of misbehavior: *Your bourbon is good enough for me.*

JD called him at home. Chase thought it must be important, but when he called back, JD just wanted to chat about Spring Break and the spring term coming up. By the end of the long, drawling, somewhat pointless conversation, Chase found himself slightly impatient.

And besides, he's apprehensive about returning to school. When he left Costa Rica, Parker's face was the sun, too bright to look at dead-on. And they talked on the phone over the remaining weeks, but it wasn't quite the same as it had been on the beach. Day by day, his ideas got tangled, bungled. He tried to picture hanging out with Parker at school—and issues sprouted. People would definitely talk about how weird a couple they are. She wasn't the girl everyone expected to see him with.

On top of that, Laine e-mailed him that she got into Deerfield for the end of spring, and her parents thought it was best. *Best. Best. What does that mean?*

He steps off the plane now in a daze, duffel on his

shouder. His cab sloshes toward Glendon, weaves through dairy farms and country homes on mute roads. It's around five when his taxi pulls through the gates, and the gray sky has smoldered into black. The snow is filthy.

He drops his bags off at the dorm, but no one's around except Jorgen, singing Coldplay in the shower. Chase strolls over to the main building, which is quiet, slowly absorbing back its tribe. The arched windows frame a wet sky, sliced now and again by black birds. It turns out that everyone's in the snack bar, and after all the back slaps and air kisses, Burns goes back to describing a stripper he's fallen in love with in Italy. Noah is egging him on. Greg's on line for a milk shake or something, and Chase is settling back into life as it had been before they'd left, when he turns to look at the stairs leading into the snack bar–

Holy fucking baby-blue coat with gold buttons.

That's Laine Hunt. Back from the dead.

When she sees him, he feels light-headed because of the expression on her face. She gained a tiny bit of weight and looks sweeter now. She looks scared, too, and she waves him out to meet her so she doesn't have to say hi to everyone at once.

"Oh my God," he says, and his face must show more than just surprise because she blushes.

"I've known for a week that I was coming back, but I wanted to sneak attack."

186

"Oh my God," he says again.

They walk outside, where the earth is sucking the snow into itself. He keeps turning to her to say something profound, but all he can come up with is: "I can't believe you're back."

They have nowhere to go, but they look good walking. As properly and formally matched as bride and groom on their wedding day.

"I know," she says. "The school gave me so much extra work in order to be readmitted, it was almost impossible. Um, I just, I don't know. I want to be here."

"I knew you would be back," Chase says, even though he didn't.

Their boots get soaked as they walk aimlessly through the brutal evening suddenly turned soft. His mind knocks back and forth like a pinball between Laine, with her angelic mouth and prim coat, and Parker, with the wise, aristocratic face and fur hat. *How does this work again?*

She sees them from her room. Something drew her to look out the window, and there they are. Her baby-blue coat and his olive moleskin Barbour jacket. Walking regally, slowly. What can he see in Laine? Honestly? Parker would like to pass one of those airport-guard wands over her body to see if it bleeps for personality. Because she's pretty sure it wouldn't.

For God's sake, the girl was made in a Connecticut factory, incubated in a glass conservatory with chintz chairs and potted orchids, trained to make cold and short and vague statements that end up seeming mysteriously eloquent but are not. In her white jeans and riding boots, no makeup, white-blond hair slicked back, she walks the grounds like a soldier, defending the perimeter of privilege.

But even from here, Laine does seem a bit like a ceramic pitcher that was dropped, that smashed into a hundred pieces, was glued together. It can still hold water, but you expect any minute for it to leak.

As for Chase, Parker keeps thinking that he's perhaps doing the gentlemanly thing and chaperoning her through this new school; since the school she showed up at in September doesn't exist anymore. Once a person has left a place and then comes back, the place no longer welcomes them the same way, or at all. Parker's mind will not yet accept the possibility that he's hanging out with Laine like this because he likes her, or he loves her. She can't imagine that he's leaving Parker in the cold. It's simply inconceivable that anyone could be so brutally unkind. But everyone has always suspected Chase had a crush on Laine.

He doesn't see Parker till Limnology class the next day. He goes to the class empty-handed, with no idea how he'll handle this, or even what he wants.

"Hey," she says brightly, nervous, as they enter the

chemical-scented classroom.

"Shit, Park. What's going on?" He gives her a brotherly hug. He senses his awkwardness and tries to act natural, his manner snowballing.

"Just back to reality, I guess."

Chase nods. He won't look her in the eye.

"How was the rest of your vacation?" she asks.

"It was good. I mean Costa Rica was amazing, but things were pretty insane at home. I'm still a little beat up." *I'm such a loser.* In his head he recounts hours spent looking at Mal Pais pictures and checking e-mail.

"Wow. I can't believe you had the energy. I went up to the mountains and stayed with my grandparents. Which is why I didn't return your e-mails at the end, I just got them by the way; they don't get Internet up there. Or even TV, for that matter."

"Oh, no worries. I just figured you were busy."

Parker slaps his arm. "Chase, I would have written you back. You know that."

"Well, you never know with you. You're quite the enigma. Thought you might have taken up with a dude with a matching cape or something."

She hits him again lightly and laughs. She's looking into him, trying to see something. "When did you get back?" she asks.

"Yesterday evening. You?"

"Same. Have you seen everyone?" This is the loaded question.

"I have." He nods then, at a loss for more conversation in the face of her new silence. Luckily the class starts.

No green grass yet—just matted, wet clumps of earth. But the rain is better than the snow. Parker is walking back to the dorm to meet Nikki for a walk into town. Town has been the savior this semester. Buying Twizzlers at the gas station, sitting in the swings on the ghost-town playground in the public park, chewing on their candy, dragging sneakers in the dirt, talking over the meaning of life.

The town doesn't belong to them, and when they're there, they don't belong to anything, and that's the point. They're not at school and they're outsiders in town. When they step across the soggy baseball diamond, with no game and no players, they can exist in someone else's hometown, steal hours from someone else's life.

Today they'll go to the pizzeria to see the kittens that were born last week. Joe, the owner's son, will take them down to the basement again, to where the feral kitties are curled in newspaper shreds in a cardboard box he'd arranged. They'll go back up, flirt with Joe and whoever else is working, eat slices off paper plates saturated with orange grease, and maybe put a few songs in the jukebox.

But when Parker approaches the dorm, Laine is waiting

there with Nikki, both of them sprawled on the big wood stoop of the dorm, the spade-shaped leaves of the lilac bushes wet with rain. Laine in a windbreaker and jeans, as if this would be a hike, not a walk.

"What's up?" Nikki says in a voice that makes Parker know she's uncomfortable with this. "You ready to hit the road, Park?"

Parker's too taken aback to make excuses. "Yeah, definitely. What's up, Laine?"

"Hey," she says with an overly polite smile. "I'm psyched to check out this pizza place. I actually never went."

"Well, it's just pizza," Parker says before she can stop herself. She's not even sure what she means.

Nikki frowns at her, privately, then says: "I told Laine about the kittens, I can't wait to see them."

"Great, cool." Parker fumes.

They walk along the road, and Laine concentrates all her energy and insincerity on Parker, asking dumb biographical questions, which Parker can barely answer. They've never really gotten to know each other, so they're going over the basics. *Is she doing this to make me cry? Or did she promise herself to give the poor Canadian girl a chance? Does she know about Chase? How could she not?*

They don't get far before Parker reaches the end of her rope. "You guys, I'm going to turn back."

The two girls look at her with surprise. They stand on

the edge of a meadow, cars occasionally whizzing by. Nikki asks why, and Parker claims she doesn't feel good.

She can feel their stares on her back as she walks along the road. Nothing seems real. She almost feels drunk, unable to walk a straight line, so disoriented by anger.

That night, Nikki pokes her head into Parker's room. "She's trying, you know," she says, after a moment.

"Trying to *what*?" Parker asks.

Nikki pauses, then says, "She doesn't know, you know."

Parker looks at her. "Well, don't tell her."

"I haven't. I'm following your strict no-interference rules," she says, and Parker wonders if she heard a note of sarcasm. She's not sure. "I just wanted to tell you."

Parker wonders, though, as she studies through the night, robotically making index cards for an English paper, if Nikki hasn't told Laine because Nikki wants Laine to be happy and doesn't want to further complicate her rocky return to school. Parker doesn't know. Her common sense careens, spirals, knocks around her big, lonely mind.

Chase and Laine are eating cereal, bleary-eyed, at a big table in the dining hall.

"How are you?" someone asks her.

"I'm okay. It's been a long couple of months though, you know?" she answers.

"Yeah, tell me about it," Chase says.

192

Laine's in a chocolate dress with riding boots, her white-blond hair longer than when she left. She scans the room. He knows she feels people talking about her.

"I mean, what *happened* after the Gold and Silver?" a girl asks now.

The mention of the night causes Laine to roll her eyes. "Ugh. It was crazy," she says elusively.

Later, as they walk across soaked fields to practice, he puts an arm around her shoulders. "Laine, it's no big deal. No one cares. We're all just glad you're back."

She still doesn't look up.

"Christ, I'm failing out of school," he says. "Burns is a drug dealer. Nikki's even wearing plaid."

Laine finally laughs.

"You see? We're all a little crazy right now." Chase stops her to push hair from her face. She smiles.

"You really helped me out, Chase, you did," she says, but can't look at him while she says it.

"Glad I could help," he says. "Figured you couldn't live without me."

"What*ever*," she answers, laughing.

They keep walking, and Chase is strutting. He's never in his life been needed, been necessary to someone, and he feels he is now. He wishes, for some reason, that JD would cross their path. So he could see what it looks like for a guy to pick himself up and move on. Chase's thoughts veer crazily from one thing to another, landing on Parker and taking off again before he thinks too much about it.

Back in the day, in first grade or so, his class played tag at recess under the big South Carolina sky. Mrs. Montgomery would stand in the shade of the cypress tree as the kids ran in the heat, touching one another, tagging too hard, hard enough to leave a red hand on the skin. They called out: *Chase, chase me,* or *Let's chase Chase.* Everyone loved the play on his name; it cracked them up, as if it was a taunt. The repeating of it over and over—his name, the demand, his name—left him as dizzy as spinning on swings.

"Hey, retard. Why are you cutting up that onion?" Chase asks Noah.

Rain is slaughtering Cadwallader—to the degree that they can hardly hear the TV—and they're sharing pizza in the common room.

"I'm throwing 'em on Burns's slice before he gets back from the can." Noah doesn't raise his head while he speaks; instead, he continues to slice.

"Why?"

"'Cause that little shit superimposed my face on a naked body and posted it on Craigslist last night."

The group erupts in laughter.

"Nuh-uh," he says, pointing his knife at them. "No laughing."

"Where can I see this? This is unbelievable." Gabriel's already standing.

"I wouldn't get so excited, Chavez. He threw a couple pics of you onto prisonpal.com," Noah says.

Gabriel's face drops.

"What's the onion for, though?" Chase snickers.

"He's allergic." Noah smiles.

Everyone stops laughing.

"Are you stupid? That's going to send him to the hospital," Greg pipes up after trying to ignore the conversation.

"Hell, I say send him to the emergency room," Chase adds. He feels people looking at him.

Burns comes back to find the half-sliced onion by his plate. "Who put this here?"

"I did, asshole, and I was going to rub it on your pizza and watch you blow up like a balloon, but I'm a nice guy," Noah says. "So take down the goddamn ad or I'll beat your ass."

"Easy, tiger. You should be *proud*. You got, like, thirty e-mails today."

"Please, like I care," Noah lies.

"What's the issue, really?" Chase says. "Sow your oats, Noah."

"Listen to Don Juan over here." Burns smirks. "Noah, you could learn something."

Noah lunges, and Burns runs for the exit.

"Jesus Christ. Those two are getting absurd," Greg says once they're gone.

"You should have heard them on the phone last night to these escort services," Chase says.

"I was there!" Greg says. "Burns was getting *foul.* Talking about tying the girls up and leaving them naked in the snow. It was eerie."

"Listen, boys," Chase starts out, using a tone of voice his dad uses sometimes with his own buddies. "You gotta lend me a hand figuring this out."

"What's the deal?" Gabriel asks.

"Oh, shite. I got two on deck. Parker and Laine." He leans back, arms crossed, seeing himself as his boys might see him now. Slightly amused by his own predicament, but also earnest about doing the right thing. Gabriel and Greg must be jealous. *I would be,* he thinks. "Dude. What am I going to *do?*"

Greg's and Gabriel's faces are straight, they betray nothing but a desire to help.

Greg gives it a shot. "That's a hard one. It really depends on which one you want, what you've said to them, or like, I don't know. What you think you owe them."

"I don't know that I owe either of them anything."

"Let's go back to what you want," Gabriel tries.

"I've always been interested in Laine," says Chase.

"Well, that's vague, my friend," Greg says.

"Parker is *awesome*, but maybe I confused her being a great buddy and being a girlfriend."

Gabriel and Greg look at each other. Gabriel offers this: "Sounds like you already know what you're doing, man."

15

JD walks into Chase's room without making a sound. He's shirtless, the sling covering his left shoulder. He's holding a Snapple bottle with the label ripped off. Tobacco spit in the bottom.

"Chase?"

Chase hadn't heard him come in and pops up from his bed.

"Sorry, man. You pulling your pud?" JD has turned his back.

"No, dude. You just scared the shit out of me." Chase keeps his voice even, but his desire to have moping, blood-brotherly conversations with this kid has faded.

JD takes a seat at his desk. "So what's been going on, bud? You've been in hiding ever since you got back."

"Just life, you know. Just living."

"How're your grades?"

Chase looks to see if JD is kidding. "Are you, like, my father?"

"Naw. I'm your friend. I'm your proctor, bro. Relax."

"My grades are *shit*, and they're none of your business."

"Easy, chief. I heard you might be having *difficulty*. I was being a friendly neighbor." He says these phrases sometimes, and Chase wants to kill him.

"Okay, Dr. Phil," Chase replies, and it's the first time he's sarcastic to JD. "How's your arm, by the way?" Chase overheard Upper-forms talking about JD playing golf at Sawgrass over Spring Break, his arm strong and flexible. Chase didn't want to believe them.

"Still banged up, you know? It's gettin' there, though." JD doesn't look at Chase.

Lately JD's been showing the steaks and pancakes he's been scarfing; he's pudgy, bloated. He goes on diatribes about how Layla's probably got a new guy at UNC, or more than one guy. How she's the best JD will ever have, he'll never get anyone better, and now she's gone. It doesn't matter that she calls him every day; he's intent on believing what he wants. Dark circles under his eyes. What once was the unspoken moroseness that made JD mysterious is now incessant oscillations between calling all girls evil and calling them saintly. Whenever Chase reminds JD that he's out of here soon, hoping to raise his spirits, JD shrinks deeper into himself, as if graduation day is the guillotine.

I have no patience for this, Chase thinks. *Get it together, man.*

"Speaking of grades, I should do some work," Chase says, although he makes no move to do so.

JD takes a long, sad look at Chase. In his eyes are uncountable things. And he gets up slowly, like an old man. He leaves the room.

Charlotte is in the library when Nikki comes over to Parker's room. Parker's lying on the bed with her Walkman and the fat earphones, old PiL music whining through. *This is not a love song.*

"Yo, babe. What's happening?" Nikki asks.

Parker looks up, and Nikki sees her eyes are red. "Hey, there."

"God, it's weird, I kind of got used to having my room to myself."

"I bet, yeah, it's got to be weird," Parker says, sitting up and raking her fingers through her messy hair. "I keep meaning to ask, how are things with you guys? Do you ever talk about Schuyler and stuff?"

Nikki stands, picks up an antique perfume bottle on Parker's dresser. "We make fun of her, you know? But that's pretty much it. I think because it's too fresh of a wound. Like, maybe we'll talk about it in a year or so. I mean, it's fucked. The girl knew they were seriously messing with my life." Nikki holds one of Parker's turquoise chandelier earrings to her own ear and looks in the mirror. "And she didn't do anything."

"It's crazy, Nik. The whole thing is crazy. It's amazing that you guys are working through it."

"How are you?"

"I'm great," Parker says.

"I mean, with everything."

Parker makes a blank face. "I'm good." She's back to keeping things to herself. The experiment in being an open book didn't go so well.

"Baby, you can talk to me whenever."

"Thanks," Parker says primly.

When Nikki leaves, she puts on her song again, lies on her back with her hair rippling around her, heart to the sky, eyes closed.

At three thirty in the morning, Burns and Noah swing open the door. Gabriel hits his head on the frame of the bunk.

"Get up, shitheads. You do *not* want to miss this." Noah shakes Chase as Gabe grabs his slippers.

"Christ, dude. It's almost four." Chase rolls over.

"C'mon, man, it will take two minutes." Noah pulls Chase's leg until he finally slides off the bed. Chase gives Noah a grave look.

Burns is waiting by the door to the first floor stairway.

"Welcome to history, gents." Burns flashes his ugly teeth. "Okay, here's the deal. Gabe, you watch the stairwell on floor one. Chase, you watch the second floor. In thirty minutes we'll meet up in my room. Cool?"

"Screw off, Burns. I'm tired as balls and I don't want to do any more of your dumb crap." Chase turns to walk back.

"Too tired, loverboy?" Burns asks. "Too tired to hang with your boys?"

"What is this?" Chase asks.

"Just stand up there for five minutes, that's all I am asking," Burns says.

"Hurry up." Chase continues up the stairs.

Chase's alarm buzzes at nine thirty. He has a sleep-in on Tuesdays and Thursdays. As he grabs his towel, he notices Gabriel still passed out in his bed.

"Gabe? Get up, dude. You're missing class."

Gabriel grabs his pillow and slides it away from his mouth as he speaks. "I'm taking a Red Card."

Gabriel has never missed a class at Wellington, let alone a full day.

"You sick?"

"Tired. Last night was foul."

Chase is quiet. There's no arguing that. "No shit. It's *Burns*. What did you expect?"

Gabriel rubs his palms over his eyes to wake himself and then climbs out of the bottom bunk. "Not a trash can of urine. Mr. Halliday's place must be destroyed."

"Yeah."

"Burns didn't even tell Noah that he left that surprise dump in the trash can as well."

Chase looks out at the bleary spring morning. Birds make the limbs of young trees bounce. Everything out there is gray and wet. And Chase feels a weight on his chest like a stone. He has never felt so overcome by something that he could not see. His skin pricks with sweat.

"Hey. Sorry, I'm late." Chase slides into an orange desk chair and tosses his bag on the table.

Parker doesn't look up. A "DIE YUPPY SCUM" pin is attached to her green military blazer.

"What's the word, bird?" he tries. He flicks her pencil as she tries to write.

"My God, you are so annoying," she says, as though to herself.

"So how are we going to work this test? I almost failed the last one since you decided to take a Red Card and not tell me. You know I can't do the multiple choice." Chase looks over and sees her index fingers resting on her temples. He smiles. "Park, you bailing on me?"

"Are you going out with Laine?" she asks in a shaky,

steely voice. He can see her fingers tremble, and she crosses her arms and tucks her hands away.

He'd known this was coming. But he'd pushed it to the farthest corner of the basement of his head, buried in an unmarked cardboard box, because he had no idea what to do. He decides now to go with Noah's plan of action.

"Listen. I've been meaning to talk to you since we got back," he blusters. "This whole thing is *super* awkward for me. You see, Laine and I had a kind of relationship, you know, by e-mail, before you and I even went to Costa Rica—" Chase feels panic build as he watches Parker's face betray surprise and what looks like disgust. "And then you didn't return any of my e-mails after we got back. I have to follow through on what I started with her, do you understand?"

Parker stands and faces him. Tears on lashes. "You know what? You know what I just realized? I don't even *like* you."

He stands, leans over, and grabs his bag, feeling the sword of moodiness suddenly gut him. "You know what? Fuck you then!" He lowers his voice after a few heads turn. Instead of walking away, he stops and drops his bag. "You walk around in your fucking cape and pass judgment on everyone."

She gets vehement. "What's wrong with my cape?"

"So then let's be friends," he says, his voice cracking with frustration.

She laughs bitterly. "You *idiot.* If I don't like you, why

on earth would I be friends with you?"

"I thought you meant, you know, like me *like that*."

"You're an *idiot*, Chase. You can be friends with the person you go out with."

"That's a recipe for disaster. How can you go out with someone you're so close to?"

"Oh my God, you're beyond."

"Tell me why you don't like me," he says now, believing he'll have to coax her into it.

But she responds after a minute, and with that childlike seriousness. "You're just so *careless*."

He pauses. "Okay, you know what? I don't know how to do this if we're going to be all honest and shit."

"You're a lost boy."

"You're a freak! You're from fucking Mars!"

"Canada."

"Exactly!"

"Come on up sometime," she says, her tears falling now as she puts on her coat and walks out. "We're better human beings."

Chase calls out to her as she slams the door: "What, are we having a geography argument here? What the fuck, Park?"

Cadwallader dormitory spends four nights and the next weekend on lockdown. Aside from classes, no one is allowed to leave the dorm. Chase and Gabriel separate themselves from Burns and Noah during the week, claiming that the group shouldn't be seen together, but Chase is simply tired, and he can feel a real rift developing.

He folds himself into Laine. Or the idea of her—even now that they're hanging out, he still can't get beyond the fantasy. Greg says he puts her on a pedestal and Chase has a vision of Laine on the cake stand his mom uses, legs crossed and swinging off the ceramic edge. At night they instant message, typing back and forth for hours. She recounts her last three months at home and Chase tells her about his family. They're living on the same acre now, but still knowing each other on the Internet.

Lovey-dovey online, yet when they see each other in person, they have absolutely no idea what to do with each other. They languish in various public places. Talk about classes, and the weather, and what people are wearing. They talk about how other people look, or who likes or hates who else, or who's rich and poor. They talk about how fucked up the school is, how fucked up the teachers are, how home is so much better, full of freedom and booze and life.

They haven't kissed yet. Laine, in fact, made it quite clear that there would be no affection in front of others. He reached for her shoulder one day in the dining hall, and she tore it away as if he'd tried to brand her with a burning cattle stamp.

He does love that everyone watches them. Two senior

guys who were friends with Reed ask him politely, with a businesslike manner, if he and Laine are together. He tells them yes. He stops short of giving them Reed's phone number and paying them to call him, to tell him Chase has the prettiest little blonde at Wellington.

One of the guys had asked him this winter, in the same officious tone, if he'd been the one to find Mary Loverwest. At least now Chase is getting attention for walking hand in hand with a girl whose heart is beating.

On a Tuesday night after study break, Chase finally walks Laine back to her dorm. This is the equivalent of a first date at boarding school. They loiter behind the wet shrubbery of Lancaster, where buds are still hard beads. He's shaking, and he can tell she is too.

"Well, I'll probably end up IMing you in an hour anyway so it's not really good night."

Laine looks up at Chase and nods. "Yeah, we tend to chat a little at night, don't we?"

Chase smiles and shrugs. "Yeah, I guess. So I'll, uh, talk to you in a bit then." Chase reaches for her hand, grabbing at the tips of her fingers.

"Yeah, in a little while. I need to work for a bit. And you *definitely* need to!"

Chase frowns and she taps his stomach.

"All right, all right." Chase leans in fast and kisses her softly.

She kisses him back and pulls away.

He tries to hide his Kool-Aid smile. "Talk to you in a bit."

"Bye, Chase."

He sails across the quad, caught in early-April winds, a dumb, lucky grin planted on his face as he stares directly at the damp sky. A quarter moon, carmelized, comes out from behind tough black clouds.

Parker gets out of the shower, having warmed her bones with scalding water. There's Laine, in a terry cloth white robe, standing at the row of ancient sinks, flossing her teeth in the mirror. The night is a vague blackness beyond the mottled glass of the window.

"Hey," Laine says awkwardly, the thread between her front teeth.

"Hey," Parker manages to say, and even gives a little wave while holding her basket of toiletries and keeping her towel closed at the sternum.

Laine's eyes follow Parker, and she can feel the turquoise laser beams burning into her pale back. And by the time Parker gets into the room, puts on her ivory flea-market men's pajamas with the stranger's initials scrawled carelessly over her heart, snaps off the light, lets out her breath finally—she's cold to the core of her ribcage.

In the dark, white snow sneaks in the window, which

they have to leave open because the radiators make the room too hot. She can hear Nikki in her mind: *Why don't you just talk to Laine?*

The very idea of talking to Laine reminds Parker of taking a crowbar to herself, breaking herself open. *I don't want to have to talk.* The other problem is that when she thinks about her complaint, namely that *she*, Parker, had been going out with Chase, she realizes this isn't true. They hooked up once in another country. Granted, she believed more had happened between them, but there's only that scrap of evidence.

Was the whole thing in her head? *This* sucks *too much to even cry about*, she thinks, fists clenched in her bed.

For some reason she thinks of Peter, New Year's Peter. She thinks about his flannel jacket and boots, the way his cuffs were unsnapped and they fluttered in the wind when he drove the Indian, dust rising like smoke. Why can't she get dizzy when she thinks about him, the way Chase makes her dizzy? She forces herself to remember his thigh between hers in the cold barn. She wants to want more.

During the winter she's gotten a few letters from him, chicken scratch block-letter notes. A mosaic of big sky and innocent news and keg parties on farms and drifts of snow. They meant something to her but not everything.

When they were ten or so, riding the school bus home one day, they licked temporary tattoos and pasted them on their forearms. Peter purposely stuck the same one onto his skin as Parker's: a blue bird. She hit him, called him a copycat, wanting nothing to do with him that way. She wonders now: *Can you ever learn to love someone you don't love? Can friends become something else? If you love someone, can you learn not to love them anymore?*

She dreams that the snow piling up is a mound of tiny, weightless chicken eggs, a couple of them dappled, some stained with nest dirt. But she knows that they're empty, and this pleases her enough to fall asleep. Meanwhile, though, they're just snowflakes melting on the carpet after they fall there. Tomorrow there will be a wet spot on the floor. It's a night she will never forget: the egg dream, the place beyond crying, and the epiphany that there is always more than one true version of the truth.

16

Spring is breaking itself out of the hard land. It's not pretty. The ground is funky, musky with rain and roots, and unrelenting.

Chase has gone from indoor mediocrity on the squash team to outdoor mediocrity on JV tennis. He drags clay into the room like cats drag litter through a house.

Chase moves from dorm to carrel, from carrel to back corner of the dining room. Keeps throwing up whatever he eats. He's way behind. He wheedled an extension out of Ms. Farley for his poli-sci paper. And if he writes three extra-credit papers for algebra, he might make up for his failed quizzes and pass the class after all. He's been *negotiating*.

He's also been *hallucinating*. Staring desperately at facts and figures, and instead seeing insects wiggling where there should be words and numbers. And when he tries to look at the real insects on the pages of his Limnology text, they take wing and vanish from the page.

He rubs his eyes now. He's at his own desk, it's one A.M. He knocks back a Ritalin without water, the bitterness drawing a chalk line down his throat. He's been taking Sonata for four-hour bits of sleep at night. It beats Ambien, which requires eight hours. Without a sleep aid, he lies in bed, feels doom swooping down on him like dark, soft birds landing on his bed, and he can't move.

He's hanging, swinging like a pendulum in half consciousness, lost in the dead center where he can't grab hold of sleep or wake himself up. A pit of dogs lolling below him, golden-fleshed things that don't even need to show a tooth to remind him that he can be unzipped from Adam's apple to groin in a heartbeat, and his life will tumble in a wormy mess from the space there.

Christ! He jolts awake, rolling into awareness, at dawn. He doesn't know where he is, or who he is, or why he is. He fumbles for the Dr Pepper bottle by his bed. He stares, eyes cloudy and painful, squinting at Gabriel's Prada loafers before he can remember what shoes are.

Burns has rigged a lock on his door for two days but Chase and Greg need more study drugs.

"You think he's dead?"

"Nah. Saw him headed over to Club Tennis on my way to the gym yesterday."

Chase scratches the door and jingles twice. Nothing. He repeats. No response again.

"Open the door, bitch!" Greg bangs loudly on Burns's door and backs away. They can hear shuffling in the room and nod at each other.

"Nice work. Very subtle."

Greg puts on a faux English accent that he got from watching Chase's *Layer Cake* too often: "He's a dodgy little minger, ain't he?"

Chase is laughing as Burns cracks the door.

"Fuck you laughing about? Thought we weren't allowed to hang out anymore." Burns is sitting wan and shirtless on his bed, the room in disarray, his frame incandescent, bones glowing through gray skin.

"Jesus Christ, dude. You look like shit." Chase backs away from the bed and toward the door.

Greg kicks over a spitter and is covering the mess with Burns's dress shirt. The room smells like armpit and meat chili, a half-eaten Styrofoam bowl of which lingers on the desk.

"Yeah, well I had to go underground after the little prank," he says like a jaded ex-con.

Greg laughs. "No shit, you think? You dumped bodily

waste into someone's home."

"Yeah, it's been a hilarious week," Burns answers sarcastically. "What can I do for you? I was about to beat off."

Greg and Chase look at Burns's computer, but the screen is blank. They know Burns's affinity for sex chat rooms where he asks Eastern European girls to insert household products into themselves on webcams.

"Got a new love." Burns pulls an X-rated Japanese comic book from his desk drawer.

"Branching out, that's good," Greg says under his breath.

"See these little fairy girls?" Burns asks, holding up the book like he was reading a bedtime story. "They–"

"We got it." Chase has already exhausted his tolerance for Burns.

"So sorry you boys don't approve. Not all of us are getting some right now. By the way, you bang Caroline yet, Greg?"

"I'm not telling your loud ass."

"I'll take that as a yes." Burns turns to Chase and smiles. "What about you, Dobbs? You punch Laine in the shorts yet?"

"I'm out of here. Give me the pills, bro."

"If either of you wants to borrow my little book, don't be shy, just ask."

Chase tosses a twenty on the bed. "Where's the

Adderall, bud? I'll take the friendly discount, as well."

"You are so *pushy*," Burns says like a matron. He opens what looks like a Dictaphone; the drugs are in the hollow space inside. "Nice, huh? Got it in Chinatown. I got a guy."

"Please, you got a guy?" Greg turns on the English accent again and pats Chase. "Probably got a mate downtown giving him a tosser for three quid, eh?"

Burns tosses Chase a bag while giving Greg the finger. Chase inspects the bag and throws it in the bottom of his shoe.

"Hey," Burns says. "Hide this in your wall and you can take ten of them." He chucks a bottle of Klonopin.

"Thanks, Burner. Have fun with your make-believe Asian schoolgirls," Chase says, and he and Greg walk out.

Greg shudders as they exit. "I got to wash my hands, dude. Who knows what I touched in there."

Chase isn't necessarily hiding as he watches the yoga class, but he'd rather not openly stare like a campus pervert. All athletes must take turns watching yoga class. *How could they not?*

Nikki and Laine move into downward dog in the big, glass-walled studio. They act in unison with the other girls, and Chase feels like he's watching an exquisite, enlightened flock of animals that was born knowing certain choreography.

The congregation of bodies holds two more poses, lean

legs extended and arms reaching. Like egrets, flying. After lying on the floor, limbs spread like star points, the girls get up and move languidly to the door.

Laine pushes her white-blond hair out of her eyes, and laughs at something Nikki says. Sunbeams cut them sideways like headlights; it's that time of day. Laine looks natural, relaxed, which will end as soon as she sees him and she gets nervous, closes up. Chase hopes one day this won't be the case. They file out.

"Nice shorts, dork." Nikki taps him on the belly.

"What's wrong with the shorts? Sorry I don't wear 'jorts' like the boys on the island." His style has always been ridiculed by Nikki: from these corduroy OP shorts to the shredded fraternity shirts from Mountain Weekend and Spring Formal, the snap-button plaid shirts, the top-siders, and the shotgun shell belt.

"Chase, if they were any higher your balls would be hanging out."

Laine tries not to laugh. Nikki walks toward the locker room.

"Your shorts look fine, Chase," Laine says, being the good girlfriend.

"Hurry up in there, you two. Noah's game is about to start," Chase says.

Laine puts up her index finger to signify one minute, Nikki raises her middle finger. He laughs.

April has dawned on Wellington. The ex-jocks and partiers are playing Club Volleyball on the green, their skin desperate for the weak sun. Trails through the woods are already more beaten. Everyone flocks to the lake, which is dotted with red cupped leaves, many promises of lilies. The apple trees near the art wing have frothy white blossoms. And games get spectators, since it's a good excuse to loll around outside.

Lacrosse is a strong boarding-school sport. Baseball for the country club set. Its roots are Native American, but its players now are mostly middle- and upper-class East Coast boys like the ones on the field.

The Wellington team is skilled and quick with the ball. Passes are whipped. Behind-the-back shots from attackmen catch Westminster's goalie off guard. The senior-heavy squad puts a beating on the away team. Noah's on the bench.

Laine, Nikki, and Chase sit on the grass, shield their eyes as they wait for Noah to play. They lounge next to the scorer's table. The crowd is decent. Families and scouts. Boarding schools have a nice pipeline to Ivy League programs for lacrosse. The pipeline extends straight through college to Wall Street. Later in life, people forget the guy trading their money is the same guy who made freshmen sniff his jock, the same guy who roared like a lion when he found out he broke a thousand on the SAT's.

"Hey, douche bag." Chase smacks number 14's helmet.

"You going in today?"

Noah turns and jabs Chase with the butt of his stick.

Nikki and Laine talk about Senior Formal and which underclassmen will be asked. Chase fades into the sun, into the grass. He enjoys listening to Laine when she's with Nikki. She opens up. She forgets he's there. Nikki keeps things spicy so they talk without a break. Laine grabs Chase's head when she sees him lay it on the grass and rests it on her lap. The sun is red inside his eyes.

Jealousy. Parker literally does see green, she knows what that means now, or a radioactive mustard-yellow, to be exact. Chartreuse.

In Costa Rica, a local surfer told her a story. He and his friends once put a scorpion on a paper towel, and then lit the edges of the paper with a match. She wonders who those friends were, and whose idea it was to set the thing on fire, and she wonders what the universe of the scorpion was like at that moment. The point of the anecdote is that, as predicted, the scorpion stung its own torso by arching its tail back. Killing itself rather than burning alive. Parker wonders if they're programmed to do so, and if it's at a certain temperature or when the flames are a particular number of centimeters away.

She feels cornered, cornered by her own self. By anger and frustration that burns on all sides, and so far she's just crouching, arms crossed over her head in meager protection, squatting down deep inside her own mind.

She's never before imagined the things she's imagining on Laine. A red stain blooms on Laine's white skirt as she stands to leave the auditorium in front of everyone. She gets hit in the mouth with a lacrosse ball while playing around on the green. She fails out, or is caught smoking with someone, or decides—after Chase breaks up with her—that she doesn't belong at Wellington after all, and she leaves for good, her tail between her legs, a confirmed failure. Because Chase breaking up with her is the linchpin for all fantasies. He sees Parker across a room, and then looks at Laine, realizes his mistake. He sees Parker across a field. He sees Parker across a table. He sees Parker. He remembers.

He stares at Laine, long and hard finally, and suddenly gets an incredulous look. He almost laughs, but is too shaken. He backs away, smiling almost bitterly, or wryly. *My God*, he says. *I'm with the wrong girl. I don't love you at all.* Laine's blue eyes cloud. Her small mouth gets smaller. Her cheeks darken in humiliation. No one's ever been so ruthlessly honest with her before.

But these thoughts are grotesque! They play inside Parker's head all the time, and in class she sits still as a monk as the show inside rolls against her will. She's ashamed of these thoughts, and genuinely surprised to have them, and feels foolish too for being at their mercy.

It's like stumbling across a porno on your family's TV. *What on earth? I didn't even know we got that channel.*

Parker avoids the mirror these days. She hustles into and out of her room, her face averted from her own face.

Chase pushes away moss clinging to the fallen tree trunk. He's supposed to be writing a paper right now on Ben Franklin, but this is the only time Laine has free. A footpath leads to this space among the tall, clicking reeds. He can hear the lake licking the rocks, but he can't see it.

"This all right?" Chase reaches into his bag and throws a green Wellington Athletics shirt over the tree so Laine can sit.

"Yeah. This is great. Good spot."

Chase lights a cigarette. Then he looks to her. "You care?" He exhales away but a breeze carries it back.

"Um. I mean, it's up to you. It would be kind of bad for me to get caught."

Chase can feel her pleading, but she doesn't ask him to put it out.

"Plus, I like kissing you more when you don't." She smiles and Chase stabs the butt on a rock. He isn't sure whether she actually enjoys their make-out sessions, and he's not sure if he does either. She's like a glass sculpture: absolutely shimmering and lovely, and impossible to hold.

Laine is a *true* beginner. It's been close to three weeks and he still hasn't seen her without her shirt. He doesn't push because he doesn't have the stomach to do so, and because of how he might perform, and what dream he might dismiss. He only hopes this makes her see him as the mature guy. A real sensitive chap.

Laine stands now, breaking away from Chase's grip, and takes off her shirt. She tucks her chin behind her shoulder and looks away. It's striking, but very strange. Her hands rest unnaturally on her waist, like a child pageant contestant who's been taught how to stand. She doesn't reach for him, but allows him to stare. Goosebumps on her skin.

"You're beautiful." Chase reaches for her, trying to act calm even though he's frightened of what she's doing, and disheartened. "But you look cold."

He wraps his sweatshirt over her shoulders. Laine actually says *ouch* when he touches her breast, and then giggles, just because it's so unfamiliar. He tries to kiss her stomach but she says "it feels weird" to her.

As they walk silently up the hill later and past the cabins, Laine squeezes his hand lightly twice. "You okay?"

"Yeah, I'm good. Glad we finally got a decent day. If the weather keeps up like this it'll be a gorgeous spring." He squeezes her hand back, unable to think of anything to talk about.

JD asks Chase if he feels like having a dip. Says he got this crazy outtake of a Steve Earle recording from his brother in the mail.

Chase gives him a friendly punch to the side of his arm.

"Yeah, buddy, I'll come up later."

Knowing he won't.

Nikki and Parker go to town on Saturday night. It's Nikki's idea.

"Just us?" Parker at some point says, embarrassed to have to ask.

"Yeah, let's catch up and stuff, get the hell out of here."

They go to the two-dollar movie place in the strip mall outside Glendon, which is dank because the place is too cheap to be heated. It plays random stuff, and they watch a seventies flick they never heard of. The dialogue is so bad they spend half the film panting with derision, laughing and trying to be quiet, so as not to disturb the one other person in the big dark room. At a certain moment, when the mean redhead is about to fall into the arms of the stupid blond guy, in some martini lounge in a wrinkle in Hollywood time, Nikki spills her box of Gobstoppers.

"Oh, shit," she whispers, and this sends them into gales of laughter, clutching the arms of their worn-velvet chairs, and the candy dances on the floor, clicking hard with each bounce, and this fuels their giggles to the end credits.

After, they go to the sad little Chinese restaurant where no one else is eating. At the bar, the busgirl and the bartender are going through tickets with a calculator. The waitstaff wear cheap satin remakes of dresses that were beautiful back home. The late snow quietly, stealthily melts outside. And neither of these two odd parties—the employees languishing at the bar, and Nikki and Parker at the corner table—belongs here in this sleepy town. The girls pour sugar onto the wet saucers of their teacups, push the mounds around with red straws. The sky outside is perfectly starless and black.

Nikki tells Parker, after the waitress delivers their fried rice, that she "tested" Laine.

"What do you mean?" Parker asks, wincing as she eats a too-hot bite.

"She has no idea of what went down in Costa, babe. How could she?"

Parker puts her fork down and gives her friend a look. "What did you say?"

"Nothing!" Nikki protests. "I said nothing."

Parker keeps staring. "You *know* I'm already too *prideful* for this, Nik. I can't take anyone interfering and all that."

"Oh, really," she says derisively, as she's been told this too many times.

"Sorry," Parker mumbles.

Nikki dips a dumpling in the soy sauce, not looking at Parker. "I said nothing. I just showed her the pictures from the trip."

"And? What did that do?"

"Nothing!" Nikki says again, looking up. "That's what

I'm saying. She just, she seemed a little surprised to see the ones with you and Chase together."

They have ginger ice cream and more jasmine tea. Nikki insists on paying, using one of her usual tricks: She has allowance to spare and it's the end of the month. Parker can't complain, because she can barely ever afford paying her share anyway. When they get back to their rooms, they part ways, flushed and peaceful. Parker puts the movie stub in her mirror frame. Nikki is the real thing, sometimes. She truly is.

17

Tiny green leaves on trees. A balm in the air, like some-one breathing out of the sky. It's a living air. Among the disintegrated leaves from last fall that spent the winter under snow and have almost turned to soil, a butter-orange crocus stands up on its crisp white stem.

The whispers of "DC" have turned into panic and after-hours speculations. Chase finally decides enough is enough. It's bedtime. But he can barely blink, let alone close his eyes for sleep. Instead, he lies on the top bunk, staring at the glow-in-the-dark astronomy stickers shaped into the profile of a girl's breast.

The news sent shockwaves through Cadwallader. Burns got brought in to answer questions. Mr. Halliday, who had it out for Burns since the trash can incident, pulled a surprise room check and found a big bottle of assorted pills with a Canadian doctor's name on the label. The Disciplinary Committee, or DC as it's called and feared, met behind closed doors earlier.

Though official word hasn't been released, everyone knows something. Nikki heard Burns ratted on Nurse Sinclair. Greg heard from Caroline Camper, who heard from a girl on her lacrosse team, that Burns copped a plea by turning in his "clients." Schuyler's been spreading the rumor that Burns's parents are going to sue. James Kilmon, a Prep in Chase's French 201 class, relayed a conspiracy theory involving the FBI. But the only thing Chase knows for certain is that his fate, and the fate of the pill-popping half of the Cadwallader population, lies in the hands of the seniors and faculty members who make up DC. However, he also suspects that if they punished or expelled anyone who's ever bought a pill from Burns, the school would be cut down by two thirds.

Laine suggests calling his parents. She mentions how helpful her stepfather was during her situation.

Chase imagines the phone call: *"Hi, Dad . . . Well, actually, yeah, not so great . . . There's a chance I may get kicked out of school tomorrow for buying drugs. What kind you ask? Have you heard of Adderall? Yes, it's for ADD. No, it's not 'speed for rich kids.' Well, yes, I guess it's an amphetamine . . . You're saying I shouldn't bother coming home? What was that? You're cutting me off? I may as well enlist?"*

No way. His dad is the last person he'd tell, and his mom a close second. She can't keep a secret from her Boykin Spaniel. He'd rather burn at the stake than make that confession.

But Burns is MIA. His parents snatched him up after the DC and brought him to an undisclosed location, as if he's part of a witness relocation program. Noah's wasting time scheming to "hunt Burns down like a junkyard dog," and judging from Gabriel's silence in the bottom bunk, he's going over the problem in his own anxious head.

Think. Think. Think. What did Burns say? How could he find out?

Chase enters JD's room without knocking. Only teachers knock. Chase knocked once on Noah's door during the first week of school and then watched him puke for a half hour because he'd swallowed his chew in panic. But JD has taken precautions, positioning his bed to buy a few seconds. It's only when Chase turns the corner around the bed that he sees JD seated on his tapestry-covered couch, playing solitaire, eating peanuts from a can wedged in his sling.

"Can't sleep, pal?" JD looks up from his cards.

"Sort of." Chase has the feeling JD was expecting him.

JD leans to toss shirts from the blue papasan chair. "Sit down, man. You're making me nervous."

Chase sits awkwardly.

JD turns his attention back to his game and flips a card. "Let me guess. You think he narced on you, right?"

"Have you heard anything?"

"You mean, what have I heard on DC?" JD says with his eyes still focused on his cards.

Chase swallows. "Yeah, that's what I'm asking."

With marksmanlike precision, JD spits into the Snapple bottle at his feet. "Burns doesn't want to take the fall on this one." JD leans back and makes eye contact with Chase. "That's common sense talking."

"Burns is full of shit," Chase sputters. "Don't they know that?"

"I don't know what to tell you, Chase."

Chase waits for more, but after a round or two of solitaire, it's quite obvious he got all he was going to get, which was nothing. He thanks JD glumly and walks out.

Chase is in second-period American History when the class is startled by the entrance of Dean Talliworth. He has forgone his bow tie for a Brooks Brothers double-breasted gray suit. He waddles up to Professor Langley and whispers in his ear. The class watches both men turn to look at Chase.

"Mr. Dobbs," Talliworth says. "A word?"

Chase's classmates watch him. As he grabs his notebook and exits, the whispering gets louder.

Chase and the dean exchange neither words nor glances as they head to the headmaster's wing. Students in the snack bar stare. Chase has been here before, but only in a recurring nightmare, one that's now coming true.

The only blessing is the silence, as it gives Chase time to index recent infractions, stuff besides the Burns hoopla that could cause him trouble. Has he finally been caught cheating in Limnology? Can he get busted for drinking or smoking when he's sober? A Rolodex of excuses spins in his mind.

When they enter the office, Ballast is waiting on Talliworth's couch.

Oh, shit. Ballast's presence means it's more than another warning.

"Chase, take a seat next to Mr. Ballast." Dean Talliworth settles into a leather chair. "Do you know why you are *here*, Chase?"

Chase fidgets on the couch, then takes a deep breath. "Can't say I do."

Ballast refuses to meet Chase's eye. Dean Talliworth flashes a smug grin. He pats Chase on the knee lightly. Chase crosses his legs to discourage additional paternal gestures.

"Chase, what if I was to tell you that one of your classmates has accused you of dealing drugs? Would you happen to know anything about this?"

Chase is shocked and relieved. *This is too ludicrous.*

Talliworth has nothing. Another bullshit rumor.

"No, sir," he says. "Look, I may not be Wellington's most esteemed student, but I don't sell drugs."

"Chase, we have come to discover that your friend Mr. Burns had been involved in distributing pharmaceutical drugs that he received from . . . from a certain source. Were you aware of this?"

Chase can sense Talliworth's confidence.

"What? No. I mean, I heard about it in the same way everyone else did. Rumors or whatever, but *I* didn't sell anything. That's, it's just not right."

Ballast puts a hand on his shoulder. "Easy, Chase. If you didn't do anything wrong then there's nothing to worry about."

This sounds as much like a threat as a promise.

"All I'm saying is, I swear to God, I did not deal. Ever." Chase wracks his brain for how he was linked to the dealings. "Who told you this? I don't believe you. You're just looking to boot me!"

"Chase, how about you calm down." Ballast stands up. "Robert, can we allow Chase back to class? You and I can talk."

Dean Talliworth stands as well, thinks for a moment before answering. "I am afraid it is not that simple. Contrary to what Mr. Dobbs may think, I do have more than just a hunch for bringing him in here. Because of this, we are performing a room search immediately."

Chase stands between the two men, uneasy as a horse before a hurricane. "Fine. Let's go." He bluffs as much confidence as he can.

Apparently word spread quickly after Chase was taken out of class because Nikki, Laine, and Greg are waiting outside the dean's wing.

"Yo, what happened? You all right?" Greg murmurs to Chase, who won't look him in the eye.

"We're going to check my room."

Greg gives Chase a hard stare, knowing there's nothing to do now, but still wishing he could do something.

Dean Talliworth nods at the three students. "This is none of your business, so please go to your next class."

Gabriel is lying in his boxers on his bed playing God of War when the door bangs open. He jumps up and tosses the controller.

"Yo." Chase nods at Gabriel. "They want to check our room. Someone told them I was selling with Burns."

Gabriel throws on a T-shirt.

"Gabriel? I think you are well aware that TV's are not allowed. Unless, of course, this is your TV, Mr. Dobbs?"

"No, it's mine, sir. I'll get rid of it." Gabriel finds flip-flops and moves toward the door.

After twenty minutes, both beds have been searched and flipped, drawers emptied, shampoo bottles sniffed, and the closet ransacked. Talliworth has found nothing.

"I think it's safe to end this procedure, Dean," Ballast says with restraint.

"One last thing, Mr. Ballast." Dean Talliworth walks to the east wall, glances at the removable plank. "Chase, perhaps you could save us the trouble?"

Chase can no longer talk. It's over. The space is jammed with Stoli and Skoal and worse, Burns's bag of pills.

"Mr. *Dobbs*. If you wouldn't mind." Dean Talliworth is sure of his victory.

Chase wants to hit him. To run. To beat Burns bloody.

But all he can see is his father's face.

Chase points to the fifth panel. "Just push it in." He sits back on the bed and looks at Ballast. Ballast tries to read Chase's face.

Talliworth rummages in the darkness of the hole. He winces, grunts. His nails scratch the inside of the cavern. Then he stands back. He shows Ballast a bewildered look. "You look in there, James."

Ballast takes his turn, reaching in and even standing on the chair to peek in. He turns to them both. Shakes his head. "Nothing."

Chase's jaw drops.

Talliworth makes a painful mouth. "Well, then. Follow me, Mr. Dobbs."

The dean walks out. Chase almost has trouble standing,

but manages to get up and looks to find an empty panel. It makes no sense. *Who cleared this out?* He hurries to catch up.

"DC meets in twenty minutes. Wait for your father at the main circle," Talliworth calls back to Chase.

A late May rainstorm wets the black Town Car coming up Monroe Drive. Chase has been standing in the rain for fifteen minutes.

Chase had no idea his father was en route, but suspects Ballast has something to do with it. He knows his father and his advisor have been talking behind his back all semester. He shakes, and the car comes to a stop. Chase can't see in the windows.

Randall Dobbs, in a blue suit, his white hair now blown straight up in the wind, exits the car with nothing more than a briefcase and barely looks at his son except to say: "Get out of the damn rain; you look like a vagrant standing out here with that damn hair."

They walk into the main building together, and Chase doesn't speak. There's nothing to say.

"I regret having to be here," Randall says.

"You really didn't have to come, Dad. It's not a big deal." Chase struggles to keep pace with his father as they walk down the marble hall, shoes leaving a trail of rain, but his father refuses to look at him.

"You think lying and drugs aren't a big deal, huh? I

wouldn't blame 'em if they threw your ass out of here."

"Dad, I didn't do anything."

They're headed to the Disciplinary Committee room. A few people lurk in the hallways but most have headed to sports practice. Chase looks at his dad's big knuckles, swollen, clutching the handle of his briefcase.

They stop outside the DC room two minutes before the meeting starts. The crew is assembled across the hall, cowering. They came for support: Laine, Nikki, Gabriel, Noah, and Greg.

"Well, this is your mess, and I expect you to fix it like a man." Randall Dobbs stares, but Chase cannot face him. Part of him wants to vanish into his father's arms the way he did as a child, and be taken away from this place.

"Look me in the eye, son. Whatever happens in there, you handle it with dignity. And for God's sake, show some remorse for your foolishness. For once I can't clean up after you."

Chase finally looks at his dad and tears form in his eyes. He nods. Randall Dobbs firmly shakes his hand and walks away.

The pair of oak doors opens and Chase can see the faces around the large boardroom table, including JD, who won't look up. A flash of red: boots. And those tights? Of course, only one person on campus wore black tights with silver spray paint splashed on them. *What is Parker doing here?*

"Chase Dobbs. You're on." Walker Jones, the student body president, pokes his head out of the DC room.

And as he walks in, Parker walks out. He smells that violet perfume. He tries to meet her eyes but she looks at the ground. She's putting her arms into her white coat, and it seems to be in slow motion. The slow motion continues as he tries to hear what everyone says to him but they sound like people talking underwater.

"Chase, did you hear me? I said, take a seat." Dean Talliworth is surrounded by four teachers and four students. Chase easily recognizes their faces. The three other deans: Dean Braden, Dean Cummings, and Dean Howard sit next to Ballast. The three students at the table beside JD are nearly as intimidating. There's Walker, his vice-president Catherine Kelter, and Matty Wallace, the student-elect head of the Disciplinary Committee. Mr. Ballast points to an empty seat across the table.

Chase looks around, his head moving as if submerged in molasses. Wood-paneled walls, twenty-foot ceilings, columns supporting the painted ceiling as in a medieval chamber. No windows, and the halogen lights are sweltering. Chase is shaking.

"Before we get started. Do you have anything to say for yourself, Mr. Dobbs?" Dean Talliworth taps a pencil on the long table.

Chase can feel the stares around the table. "I'm not sure

why I'm here. I didn't do anything."

"Then you have nothing to worry about," Ballast says.

"Mr. Dobbs, are you familiar with the Green Book we have here at Wellington?" Dean Braden begins the interrogation.

"Everyone is."

Dean Braden opens the Green Book to a specific page. "Could you read this paragraph for us, please?" She points to the top paragraph and passes the paper pamphlet across the table to Chase.

"'Any student found in possession or under the influence of alcohol or illegal drugs will be expelled.'"

What did Parker tell them?

"And would you please read the paragraph beneath that one, Mr. Dobbs?"

"'The Wellington Honor Code prohibits dishonesty, theft, and cheating. Any student discovered to be lying, stealing, or cheating will be punished accordingly by the Disciplinary Committee.'"

As if on cue, Dean Talliworth takes over. "Now that we are clear on the rules, and since it appears you are still befuddled as to why you are here, allow us the privilege of telling you. It has been brought to our attention that you were involved in selling prescription drugs to fellow students. This is a very serious matter, Mr. Dobbs. So let us ask you clearly, have you ever sold prescription drugs to any other student at Wellington?"

"No. I never have." Even though Chase knows he's innocent his voice cracks. "I never did. I promise. And I can't believe I'm going to have to tell my father you all are accusing me of selling drugs." He looks to Ballast for help and can't hold back the tears.

"Chase, we believe you," Ballast says calmly. "We just needed to hear it directly from your mouth. When a student accuses another student of something illegal, we have to hear both sides."

"Is that all? Can I leave now?" Chase makes a desperate plea.

"One other thing, Mr. Dobbs." Dean Talliworth isn't finished. "Have you ever received any illegal prescription drugs from another student here at Wellington?"

Chase's mind speeds. *What a general question to ask. How would they have any proof?* He thinks of the infirmary. Of Burns buying from the nurse. Of the pills Burns tossed to Chase, with Parker lying in the bed beside him. *That's why they brought her in here.* Chase looks over at Mr. Ballast, hoping that he'll say something before he has to. *But would she really narc on me? Is she that pissed?* He looks down at the Green Book.

"Yes, I have."

"Okay, Mr. Dobbs." Dean Talliworth starts tapping the pencil again. "You are excused. You can go see your father now."

Gabriel, Greg, and Noah are the only ones waiting outside when Chase exits the DC room.

"Hey, how did it go?" Noah asks.

"Look, I gotta find my dad. Is he outside?"

Gabriel speaks up: "He went to the headmaster's office while you were in there."

Chase takes off down the hall and doesn't look back.

Outside the rain has picked up and Chase can hear it beating on the roof. As he crosses the quad, the Lincoln Town Car pulls down Monroe Drive. Chase waves but the car keeps going. The mud and rain soak Chase's suit pants as he runs down the golf course after the car and onto the commons. When he sees Parker on the far end of the quad, he yells her name. She looks up. He doesn't know why she did what she did or what he'll say to her. His hair is slicked, his wet suit flapping in the wind, his ankles dark with mud. He wants to run over to confront her but he remains still. She stares for a moment and walks away.

In his room, Chase shivers, tries to regain a sense of reality. He stares blankly at his desk. An IM pops up on his screen. Chase reads the words aloud. He doesn't know whether to cry or laugh.

Buddy,

    Borrowed your iPod and a few other things as well. Hope you don't mind that Gabe showed me where you stash it. Bout time you cleaned your room, wasn't it?

    See you around.

    —JD

Chase takes off his shoes, gets in bed in his clothes, smearing mud on his sheets, his damp hair soaking his pillowcase. He tries to get warm.

18

After sleeping through first period, Chase hurries to the snack bar, the best starting place to track down Parker. He scans the room.

"Have you seen Parker?" Chase asks Nikki.

"Haven't you bothered her enough?" Nikki sounds pissed, picking sesame seeds off a bagel.

"Well, she fucking narced on me; what the *hell*?"

Nikki gives him dead eyes. "She told the mildest version of the truth, you asshole, and you didn't even deserve that."

"Seriously, Nik, I need to talk to her."

Nikki takes a bite, wipes a tiny smear of cream cheese off her lip, then shrugs.

"Appreciate it," Chase says with some sarcasm.

He decides to check the library before hitting the art buildings. Chase sees Parker in a glassed-in study room on the second floor. She's facing away from the door, but her Timbuktu bag and sideways ponytail are dead giveaways. *Thank God she's alone.* Chase raps a knuckle on the glass until Parker turns. Chase waves and tries turning the doorknob but it doesn't move. It's locked. Parker doesn't move either. Chase points at the handle and mouths, *It's locked.* Parker watches.

Chase decides to give it a shot. He mouths to her with impatience: "Listen, we need to talk."

Parker looks down at her work.

He debates whether to ask his next question but decides to risk it, knocks again. "Could I call you later on, so we can work this out?"

She doesn't turn back to him, and he leaves, throwing his hands in the air in exasperation.

Parker puts her head on the desk once he's gone. He's a prince with a dented crown, a bloody lip, a black eye. God, walking by the kid yesterday, as she exited the room and he entered, she could smell fear on him, like sulfur. This whole experience has been surreal. From her inquisition in Talliworth's dark office, where she fixated on an ivory giraffe on his desk, its body greased and browned with years of handling, as Talliworth tried eighteen different ways to make her say Chase was dealing drugs, to the cold roundtable in the DC room, where she repeated her small, contained truth:

Burns dropped a few pills on Chase's bed in the infirmary. Chase seemed surprised. Chase gave him no money. Chase said to her, "That kid is crazy" at the time. He examined the marking on the pills. He said, "I don't even know what these are; it's probably some antidepressant," and he laughed. To my knowledge, he has never dealt anything to anyone. In my opinion, Chase barely knew Nurse Sinclair before we got sick. And while we were in there, there was no transaction done between them. Yes, he and I were barely separated during that time. We spent the whole time together. Yes, we spent the whole time together.

Why didn't she say she saw nothing? Because she didn't feel like lying. And because, in her mind, by telling a small truth, though it incriminated him in terms of accepting drugs, it made it likely that she was telling the truth on the larger issue of whether he dealt drugs, or bought them from the nurse.

But maybe her heart was being a grifter, a hustler, acting honest and earnest while really taking this chance to hurt him. She pictures her heart in a dark suit, smoking a cigar, simmering in insincerity. Parker doesn't know if she likes herself right now. She's caught in a purgatory between Dignified and Heartbroken, a place where many a girl has been stranded before. It's a place where many make mistakes.

These pills. So little and so meaningful. She imagines them flying in an arc as if tossed into a fountain, like pennies, worth any wish you can dream.

The JV tennis match against Loomis Chaffee is going better than expected. Forsythia blazes just beyond the courts, and it's a warm day so students and teachers hang out and watch. Ms. Jameson's white Labrador drools at the sight of so many tennis balls. Wellington is up 5 to 4 and Chase is serving to close out the final match. He's fought his way back after being a set down against an overweight red-headed Loomis player. Before the match started, Chase figured he'd bagel him, but the big guy's serve and whipping topspin forehand have compensated for lack of mobility.

"Forty-Love!"

It's been two days since the DC meeting, and the committee is still calling in students on Burns's list of buyers. The situation has the ambience of a witch hunt, and the longer it continues, the more absurd it seems.

"Out!"

"What!" Chase sneers, as the ball was obviously in.

The guy's been pissing off Chase with calls all day, and Chase made up his mind there's no way he'll lose to this asshole. It's been a heated match and both players have been told to settle down by their respective coaches. For some reason, Chase has it in his head that if he can win *just one fucking match*, he might not feel so much like he's drowning in thin air.

But it's not just the redheaded monster causing Chase angst. Chase keeps checking the stands for Laine. She said she'd watch, but it's not till the end of the third set that she appears on the grassy hill.

Chase holds his serve and after obligatory handshakes, he walks toward Laine as the rest of the team heads to the locker room. She's sitting Indian-style in green Puma shorts, a T-shirt, and Adidas sandals. Chase removes the headband that keeps his hair out of his face and as a joke tosses it in Laine's lap, and she brushes it off without laughing.

"That Loomis player was a dick." Chase plops down beside Laine. "You know he called me for a foot fault. Can you believe that?"

"But you won. That's the best payback, right?" Laine says, squinting in the other direction.

"I guess." Chase lies back on the grass. "Man, I've been on edge recently. I've got to relax." Chase looks over to Laine, his wet hair sticking to his cheek. "Where were you? Why didn't you show up earlier?"

"Yeah, sorry. I was swimming laps."

"It would have been nice to have you here, you know."

Laine looks down, picks at her flip-flops. "Chase, what are we doing?"

"What do you mean?" He'd rather bang his head against

his tennis racket for an hour than answer this question.

"I mean, some days you're sweet and act like you're dying to have me around and then others, you act all distant, almost as if you don't like me." Laine stares at Chase, who rips up a blade of grass and twiddles with it.

"I don't know what you're talking about," he lies. He knows he's been a headcase.

"What's going on with you?" Laine hasn't shifted her gaze; still waiting for an answer.

He finally looks up and shrugs again.

Laine takes a deep breath. "Chase, I think we should take a break. I mean, with exams coming up, it might be best if we're not distracted. We can't risk screwing up."

"Are you serious?" Chase asks. He thought they had problems, but not ones that couldn't be negotiated. His voice rises. "I think you don't want to be associated with me because I'm having, like, issues with DC and whatever. How about when you were going through all that shit at home? I was a *hundred* percent there, was I not?"

"I didn't know I owed you." Laine crosses her arms over her knees and looks in the other direction, as though restraining herself from saying more.

Chase reaches a boil and though he knows what he's about to say will hurt, he can't hold it back. "I should never have e-mailed you."

"Yeah, Chase, I wish you hadn't. Especially on Valentine's

Day. It sucks being sloppy seconds, you know."

She's staring at him now with those blue eyes, eyes he's spent months remembering, but they looked at him in a different way when he dreamed about her. "Do you have anything else you want to tell me?" she continues.

Chase knows a loaded question when he hears one. "No-o-o," he says slowly.

"I saw the pictures from Costa Rica. You and Parker hanging out and whatever."

Laine gets up and Chase doesn't stop her. He doesn't even watch as she walks away. Instead, he picks up his racket and stares at the strings. His head throbs, not with a sharp pain but a dull ache. Like he just got finished with a three-hour final exam, the exam of his young life, and he's failed miserably.

"I'm sorry," he calls out, just as she's passed out of hearing range.

He lets his head hang back and he glares with fury at the sky. The moon is out, way too early, and it's almost full. The same white as the clouds, and devoid of its nighttime glory. A moon can't glow in a baby-blue sky. When he gets up, he realizes the damp ground has soaked his tennis shorts, and he walks back to his room, stained.

19

Seventy-degree days hit Wellington as finals begin. The seniors are over school. The majority have calculated the exact grade they need on each exam in order to pass. Senior Grass is a watercolor of mesh lacrosse shorts, bikini tops, and water fights. Underclassmen study beneath the elms and maples. Upper-forms are locked in dorm rooms and the study nooks deep in the library. They whisper to themselves, sighing deeply when they miss a practice problem, lobbing pencils at students laughing in the next study room.

Upper-form spring is the time when the best plan to get better and the worst pray for miracles. Returning home with your third-year grades means there are no more excuses. It's time to tell your folks Ivy League isn't going to happen but you hear that Rutgers is *really* on the rise.

Chase studies in his room, but the words in his Limnology notebook are in Parker's handwriting, amplifying his ADD. It's been a week since the DC, and they're *still* meeting with students. The chance that DC might boot him makes it that much harder to care about studying. And how the hell can he concentrate now when earlier, in the cafeteria, he saw Laine laughing on line with Parker, who was making garnishes for their lemonades out of fruit salad. They looked relaxed, as if each of their episodes with Chase will be jokes at senior parties when they play the "Whatever happened to that kid?" game.

Chase's door swings open.

"Where you been?" Greg says, in a Nike shirt and mesh shorts, smiling, eye sockets dark violet from sleep deprivation. Gabriel hovers behind him in tennis whites.

"Keeping a low pro and trying to study so I can get the hell out of here without killing someone." Chase feels like he hasn't spoken to a friend in days and wonders if they can hear the anger in his voice.

"Relax, Drama." Greg sits on Chase's La-Z-Boy, which is lost under clothes.

"Just not sure how I could go so wrong, man. I blew *everything* this year. I blew it all."

"Chase, go *easy*, man. We *all* had our ups and downs, kid. Remember when Noah drank that bottle of Robitussin and freaked out and thought he was on fire, and you stayed up all night to keep him from calling his parents? Or when Gabriel pissed the bed after whippets in the music wing and you didn't tell anyone?"

"You told Greg?" Gabe asks, surprised.

"That's beside the point, man." Greg's on a roll. "Please. Think about Parents Weekend. I single-handedly lost the football game. And we all hung out that night, watching *Jackass* or some shit, and I wouldn't talk, but you all kept after me till I found a sense of humor."

"Well, this is a nice year-end countdown and shit, but I screwed up on a different level," Chase says.

"You did," Gabriel muses.

"I mean I fucked *up*, guys." Chase can feel his throat closing. "I'm fucking gonzo, man. And you know what, who cares, right? I mean, why should I be miserable here when I was perfectly happy at home?"

"Were you perfectly happy at home?" Gabriel asks in a seemingly innocent way.

Chase glares at him.

Greg shakes his head. "Listen. I'm not going to tell you what to do, bro, but you should think your shit through, think about what you did, how you did it, how you could have done it." Greg stands and pats him on the shoulder. "You're just throwing in the towel; it's stupid."

"This place *blows*," Chase says glumly.

"Test time for me," Greg says. "I *can't* take this place for granted, bro. Peace."

"Ouch," Chase says to him.

Greg holds out his hands in apology, saying: "Sorry, I couldn't sugarcoat it. Gabe, you coming?"

Gabriel's staring at Chase. "Hey, buddy," he says. "Have you talked to Parker?"

This is out of left field. Gabriel never gets involved in girl matters. "Not really. She didn't come to class this past Friday. I think the narc is trying to avoid me."

"I wouldn't be that pissed at her if I were you," Gabriel says, almost apologetically, looking to Greg.

Chase feels condemned, particularly because he knows if Gabriel speaks up, things are serious. Suddenly, Gabriel's and Greg's eyes meet, and Chase knows that his buddies have actually been talking about his situation. *And why the hell are they taking sides with Parker?*

"Listen, Parker told the truth, and in a way she covered your ass," Greg says.

"Fuck you guys. I don't need this lecture." Chase stands and heads toward the door but Greg blocks his path.

"In a weird way, Parker's believable because she didn't act like you were a saint," Gabriel says.

Chase stares at his dirty floor, the collage of socks and candy wrappers. He looks up at them. "Yeah, but do you really think she, like, orchestrated that? I mean, I don't think she went in there and was like, *If I tell it like this, he'll get off.*"

Greg shakes his head in exasperation. "Man, she went in there and told the truth. She could have told them about lots of other stuff you've done, but she didn't. God knows, the girl don't owe you. That's all."

Gabriel and Greg leave the room, giving him chagrined looks over their shoulders.

Chase calls his mom that night. It's a cool evening, and everyone has their windows open. The scent of crab-apple blossom comes through the halls. He feels childish for making this call and stupid for asking, but he does anyway.

"Remember when you said, I, uh, I was . . ." He clears his throat.

"Yes, honey?" she asks.

"You said I would be, um, teething this year. I was just wondering, when did Reed get his teeth in? I mean, did his Lower-form year suck like this?"

She laughs lightly, and then sighs. "Oh, baby. I love your brother, I do. But Reed hasn't even *started* getting them in."

Parker's studying Limnology on the third floor of the library, crammed into a leather chair between shelves of World War II history books. The sun pouring through the glass is hot as an oven.

She's looking at notes from the last group outing, where Frederick showed them naiads of dragonflies molting on the bank. Everyone watched as Frederick searched, shoes sinking in the mud, parting grasses with a stick.

"Ah, there," said the teacher, her skirt hiked as she crouched deeper to point. "See this dark green guy here?"

Everyone crowded and nodded.

"See the darkening of his wing pads under the skin?" she asked. "That means this is his last period between molting. What's a period between molting called?"

"Instar," a few students answered.

"Why does he have to molt?" she asked.

"Because his skin is also his skeleton, and it can't grow with him."

"What does the darkening of wing pads mean?"

"His wings are ready under the skin."

"Where will his maiden flight be?"

"To the forest."

"Why won't he stay at the lake, where he'll eventually find prey and make his life?"

"He's too weak in the beginning."

It was the call-and-answer ritual of teacher and students, performed at the water's edge. Parker looked at the naiad, an aquatic thing that couldn't breathe air, pulling itself onto the sludge of the bank. What a strange moment, in between its existence as a dully colored, underwater creature and its birth as an air-breathing iridescent dragonfly.

"Look at that!" Frederick said, as the thing wriggled. It was coming out of its last skin, the exuviae, a word Parker fell in love with.

If it's one of the vocabulary questions, she'll get it for sure. *The exuviae is what you leave behind.*

Tuesday, there's a note in Chase's mailbox to come to Ballast's office after lunch. After suffering at a crowded table, staring at an overloaded cafeteria tray that he's unable to diminish, Chase heads toward the English wing to meet his fate.

Ballast is sitting at his desk with papers in front of him. "Come in, Chase, and sit down."

Chase sits down without saying a word. Since the DC meeting, Ballast and Chase haven't talked much.

"All right, Chase. I'm going to give it to you straight."

Chase looks at the linoleum floor. *I'm gone. ROTC, here I come.*

"The DC decided that they're going to let you stay. I'm not sure why, to be honest, because on top of your academic record, any wrongdoing is enough to set you free at this point." Ballast leans back, hands latched behind his head. "But I suspect the list of students who allegedly bought pills from Burns is so long they can't take action against all of you, which means they'll take action against none of you. Half of you have your own prescriptions for the stuff anyway, which makes it all the more confusing. It's also hearsay; no one would corroborate that you bought pills from him. On top of that, the hurricane of PR could kill Wellington, literally."

"Really?"

"So . . . they're putting you on general probation, which means if you so much as sneeze in the wrong direction, you're gone."

Chase's eyes light up with dismay, joy, relief.

Ballast leans forward in his chair. "Consider yourself very lucky, Chase, and also know that out of your nine lives, you've got about a half of one left."

Chase tries to say "I will" but Ballast cuts him off.

"I know you might feel like folks are against you, but you have a lot of great people who want to see you succeed. Who are willing to go to bat for you. Who know you've got a good soul. Just remember to use it, okay?"

Chase nods. He wonders about his father's visit to the headmaster's office during his DC meeting. *Did that have anything to do with this?* He'll never know.

"Now, get out of here before I remember how pissed off I am."

On his way out, a thought occurs to Chase and he turns. "What about Burns?"

"Burns isn't coming back," Ballast says as he shuts his office door.

Chase looks at the door, has the urge to knock and thank him again, but he thinks Ballast is done for now. *Christ, what do you do when someone saves your ass? Send him a fruit basket, some long-stemmed roses?* Chase slowly, reluctantly turns away.

Walking through the main hall, which is crowded already with family of graduates and swarming with students, Chase can see only Burns, or the memory of him. In his trench coat, looking like a junior CIA member with his hideous, five-hundred-dollar ties. His scrawny face that screwed up more when he smiled, so his smile made him look like he was in pain. Burns pissing his initials in the snow. Burns carving bad words on his own wall. Like an animal that dirties its stall against all genetic instinct.

But now that he's leaving, and Chase can't imagine where or if their paths will cross again, his image triggers a dark sadness. Now he remembers the long winter afternoons, tossing a football in the Cadwallader lawn with numb fingers, the snow lit by pink sun. Dipping in Burns's room and looking through vintage playing cards Burns got from his uncle, with pictures of Marilyn Monroe on the backs, barely dressed in diaphanous layers of yellow silk. He thinks of the long letters Burns got from his nanny, written in spidery script, and perfumed. *It's so strange. We knew each other and now it's done. We won't know each other again.*

Noah tells him that night that he saw Nurse Sinclair—no longer an employee of Wellington—at the town playground, pushing her daughter on the swing. Noah waved but she didn't wave back.

20

Chase sits in room 115 in Watkins Science Center. Three days of night-and-day studying and the Limnology exam is here. He watches Randolph Casing take frequent bathroom breaks; his study outline is probably wedged between paper towels in the dispenser. He watches classmates file out, some finishing in less than an hour. Parker doesn't look in his direction. He's so tired and strung out, he keeps seeing his own head on the diagrams of nymphs and caddis flies, or his name in italics where their name should be written.

He can't stop thinking about one day in the woods, when he and Parker hiked out to a cabin. She wore her motorcycle boots and a fedora, her hair in a long braid, and she walked like a tomboy through the brush. She found a big walking stick, and pointed things out to him with it: initials carved into a beech tree, an old label-less bottle in the crook of a trunk. She's an outsider, but God knows she learned the heart of the school better than anyone, if the heart was, in fact, this wild place in the woods.

And they sat in the cabin till almost dark. The best thing about Parker Cole is her laugh. She has the longest, most sincere laugh, throws her head back, hair spilling, unselfconscious. Her long fingers tucked between crossed thighs, one leg kicked up. The tone clear and strong.

Listening to her laugh was like watching a clumsy bird who seemed wing-clipped swoon out and cut through the sky without even trying.

Chase asks Greg to come with him. When he explains why he's doing it, Greg gives him a skeptical look.

"This is downright biblical, bro. You're making a statement *now*?"

But Greg doesn't hesitate to walk with him on the sunny road into town. Greg's his most formidable friend, and it feels natural at the end of this year to have his last day be with him. Noah, he's always there, he's a goofball, he's got your back. But it's purely a comfort friendship, not a challenging one. Gabriel, he's coming to *be*. Gabriel's still not sure who he is here, who he'll be at Wellington, who he'll be in the United States. Elsewhere, even on the phone with his family, Gabriel talks faster, laughs easier, his voice goes up and down as he tells stories. It's like he still has to get his confidence out of customs, as if it's being held like quarantined cargo.

Ironically, Greg and Chase probably fought more than Chase did with any other guy this year. Chase once brought up how hard Greg must find it to belong to two groups at the school, the black crew and the white crew. *Come on, man,* Greg had said. *I already read that pamphlet. I already saw that movie. Next.* But when Greg goes buck-wild angry at anyone who tries to talk about race or class, Chase insists that everyone has a right to discuss it, it's not Greg's private property, and that there can be no changes made in the world if anyone born privileged isn't allowed to be honest.

One of the only things Greg ever said to Chase that Chase couldn't get past was after one of those arguments: *You're the white entitled motherfucker, Chase, that angry black PhDs all over this country are writing books about. It's not just that you don't know how much you got, it's that you don't even look, bro.* But that sound byte is part of the impetus for Chase wanting to walk into Glendon now, on asphalt baking in the New England sun, to the barber shop on Main Street. *I have to know what I have,* Chase thinks.

It's trapped in a place, a time warp, with the candy-striped pole out front, and inside a jar of scissors and black combs in disinfectant liquid. A solitary man in a white apron. Mr. Yeltin has an elaborate, decadent Russian accent, and the gruffest, most belligerent way of showing affection, sneering and jabbing with fat fingers at his client. The light in the room is bluish, like the air of a day or room remembered, and they all stop kidding and bantering as Mr. Yeltin holds the scissors to the gold hair, and he meets Chase's eyes in the mirror, silently asking if he's sure. Chase nods imperceptibly, and the scissors make a brutal, metallic slicing noise. A long lock of straight hair falls to the linoleum.

Greg can barely walk on the way home, he's folded over cackling, roaring with laughter, as Chase walks stoically in the sun, not looking left or right.

"Oh, shit," Greg says, stumbling, almost drunk with derision, into the dandelions on the shoulder. "Is it your birthday, kid? Going to Chuck E. Cheese? Are you gonna meet the other fifth-graders for some street hockey, Chasey? Huh? Shit, I think I seen you on a missing notice on a milk carton."

"Anytime you want to shut your mouth would be fine with me," says Chase, staring straight ahead, mullet ruffling in the breeze.

"I think you getting a mercy buzz when we get back. I'm dead serious, bro."

And that's what happens. Chase sits in a chair in his

messy, disassembled room, and Greg takes his clippers to the rest. Greg's big hand is efficient and kind, clutching his skull. Chase watches the process in the old mirror that's speckled with age, a mirror that's seen more than one transformation.

"Okay, Private Dobbs, you're done," Greg says quietly, standing in shards of hair.

Chase knows then that Greg is more of a brother to him than any blood sibling.

Kiva, whose parents have come from New Delhi to see her graduate, have arranged for a balloon ride, and Kiva invites Aya and Parker. They pack into the rental car and drive to a field where their balloon is standing, sandbagged and tethered to the earth.

They make nervous and anticipatory conversation, awkwardly stepping into the giant wicker basket. The ropes are thrown from the rising craft, and fire roars like a flower into the rainbow-patchwork silken bulb. They sway into the sky. No one says anything much—they grin, stupidly, ecstatically, amazed at the quiet and the breadth of land.

Kiva's in a lime-green sari and her mother in pomegranate. The silk flutters. The father has a waxy mustache and a black suit. The sky's been flickering gray and sunny all day, but the sun is properly out now and unwavering, its gold spilled all over the meadows down there, trickling down

hills and through yards, over farmhouses, and even cours-
ing around Wellington's tidy buildings and commons and
sports fields and church, which they see now.

"Look at that," Kiva says solemnly, strands of her raven-
black hair rising in the wind.

It's strange to see it integrated with the world, a piece of
land annexed to other pieces of land. Parker always felt it
existed separately, a kingdom with electric walls.

Somewhere down there, under a roof, crossing a green,
smoking in some woods, is the first boy she ever fell in love
with. Tiny as a plastic toy, hidden in the fortress of the
school. Her eyes are puffy already, and she doesn't feel like
crying any more so she won't. But she knows she lost him.

Kiva and her mom hold hands, which no American
mother and daughter do at this age. Parker looks at their
joined hands, and at the stuttering trumpet of flame, and
at a crow coasting beneath them at almost the same
speed, which makes it seem as though both the balloon
and the bird are languid, flowing and floating in the air,
easy in the sky.

The night before graduation, seniors used to sneak out for
a naked, moonlit Sunfish race across the lake. It was innocent, and overlooked by the faculty. But a few years back,
someone brought aboard a keg and a nitrous tank, and a
number of boats—not to mention students—got wrecked. It

was reportedly a vision: a midnight lake, water moccasins swerving over the still surface, plastic cups floating, and skinny-dipping, ecstatic swimmers, ending a chapter of memories in the dark. The seniors who took the fall were expelled the next morning in an emergency DC meeting, while their confused parents and grandparents waited at the graduation ceremony.

Even Reed called Chase last night to warn him: "Whatever you do, man, do not fuck around the night before graduation. It's bad karma."

But right now, Chase doesn't feel like partying and even questions whether he'll attend the ceremony tomorrow. Chase stuffed the army-issue duffels, hand-me-down luggage from Lieutenant Dobbs, and is sitting at his desk staring at his empty room.

Outside you can feel shrill excitement and anxiety in the balmy air, the preparations for good-byes. Everyone's going to dinner, crossing the twilit lawn together. The year seemed to last forever, and it also seemed to go by in a day and night. He went to sleep, he had a dream, and now he's going home. He thinks back to when he arrived, and the leaves were on fire, and the buildings were gigantic and foreign, their hallways like secret paths to places other students had gone before him. It goes by too fast, he thinks with panic, it goes by so fast.

Chase tears pages from Gabriel's notebook. He's going

to write a letter. He rubs his bare head, which feels strange, and thinks.

> *Dear Parker,*
>
> *The first time I saw you, last September, you were trying to get into your mailbox for the first time. You looked at the slip of paper in your hand, and then tried the combination again. You pushed the glasses back on your nose. You were embarrassed that you couldn't make it work, and you kept looking around, kind of covertly, and then you'd try again. You were too shy to ask for help. You had on that weird zebra blazer or something, and I remember a hot-pink rose in the lapel, you must have stolen it from the headmaster's garden. And it was dying. Finally you turned away from the box, and I saw you had tears in your eyes.*
>
> *I wish I knew then what I know now. I wish I'd known to stop you from leaving, and to make a little joke to make you feel better, and to help you get the lock open. I wish I'd known enough to know you, Parker Cole.*
>
> *We don't get a million chances.*
> *Love,*
> *Chase*

Graduation falls on June third. Mercedes and SUV's are parked on the quad. Behind the dining hall is the senior picnic, all the tables covered with gingham cloths, the centerpieces of daffodils trembling in the breeze. As usual, a new scandal keeps everyone on edge. Diego Caroles, a senior, has cut too many classes in his last semester and will not be able to walk with his graduating class. His family already arrived from Miami just to watch their son graduate. Chase can sense the tension between the faculty and students as he passes by. He watches the students argue with their parents about responsibility and character.

Dick Covington, Schuyler's father, lays down a takeout bag from Sullivan's Garden for his family. They snack on Styrofoam plates of salad, granola, and Smart Water. Hot dogs and hamburgers are no L.A. diet. His BlackBerry beeps throughout the meal. Their West Coast "show-me" money sparkles like a Rolex against the seersucker matte of East Coast "hand-me-down" wealth, in the form of MK's family seated next to them. They quietly drink iced tea and eat hamburgers. MK's father's blazer is embroidered with the Linx Club insignia, and her mother is in slacks and tortoiseshell glasses.

Chase smiles sadly at Schuyler as he passes by. Schuyler winks.

Kofi Annan is the guest speaker. He speaks of a global future and the social responsibility of the next generation. He speaks to seniors who are naked underneath their gowns. Seniors who are stoned or drunk so they can breathe freedom into the headmaster's face as their diploma is finally handed over. Lake Dory glitters behind the podium, its navy-blue diamonds blinking and vanishing.

Wellington has been blessed with an early summer day. Hundreds of white chairs are lined up behind the 127 seniors. Little brothers and sisters are kicking soccer balls and playing tag at the edge of the woods. Underclassmen are taking pictures from the lawn and talking to former graduates who have reappeared.

Chase marvels at the scene as he sits overlooking proceedings from the Cadwallader roof. The alarm went off when they opened the emergency exit, but no one bothers them. This is the faculty's day; another stellar year as forty-eight graduates will attend Ivy League universities. Chase sits beside Gabriel, Greg, and Noah as they share cigarettes and comment on the departing seniors.

"Can you imagine Pickford in college?" Greg looks down as Timothy Pickford, the senior known as "Standards" for his poor choice in women, grabs his diploma.

"Let's face it, half these kids are going to be tremendous losers next year. They were losers here, there just weren't enough people to tell them so." Noah smiles as he watches Pickford leave.

"I just can't believe he got into Vanderbilt. The kid is a moron," Chase chimes in.

Noah smiles. "Dude. The guy's from Nashville. His dad is the head surgeon at the hospital. There was never any doubt."

Chase nods his head as if he should have known.

For the remainder of the ceremony the guys say little. They watch enemies, bullies, crushes, friends, and role models move on. The seniors will all leave campus in the afternoon and that will be it. They'll head to senior parties throughout the eastern seaboard. They will throw up in pools in Southhampton. A few will have sex in the phosphorescent ocean in Watch Hill. Long-standing grudges will be decided with sloppy punches and empty threats on a ferry to Martha's Vinyard. There will be DUI's on I-95 and someone's parents will realize that their angel does drugs at a house on Cape Cod. Girls will skinny-dip and guys will hoard condoms. There will be three break-ups, two threesomes, and one guy will finally come out of the closet and head home on a train. Then they will all disappear.

There is no town to return to, no local watering hole to bring them back together. In five years they will return for a reunion that will last a couple days.

Chase watches as Schuyler curtsies to the audience after she receives her diploma. Her parents snap pictures of Schuyler in her white dress, a white rose pinned into her tawny hair, with that secretive smile, and hips that roll as she crosses the stage. She squints at the world as though she is looking at the sun, and Chase wonders what, in fact, the girl sees. It's bizarre to think they were lying next to each other once, bodies touching, skin touching, in the dark. It's like a story someone told him about people he doesn't know. It's like a rumor. It's like an unbelievable lie.

"Fucking Schuyler Covington. Jesus." Chase can barely get the words out.

Greg sits beside him, feet dangling. "Yep. Crazy year, right?"

Everyone nods but says nothing more. Chase can only imagine what is going through Parker, Laine, and Nikki's minds as they watch girls like Schuyler and MK move on.

Chase focuses on JD as his name gets closer and closer to being called. JD's father stands at the periphery in a pin-striped suit without a tie. He holds the hand of what someone tells Chase is his fifth wife as she wipes away tears. When JD's name is called his classmates clap and call out nicknames: "J Bird" and "Country J" and so on.

When Chase met JD's father earlier, Mr. Wanner came off as a man with everything but pride, and he wore a smell of outsiderhood like body odor. He shook Chase's hand and said: "You must be the apprentice JD told me he had this year." At which point JD turned crimson and looked away from Chase. Chase thinks he knows now why JD fell apart this semester. Plain old fear. Fear of the world, of leaving the known territory, of making it out there.

Of being a man.

So Chase looked at Mr. Wanner. "Yes, sir. JD was my mentor. He looked out for me. In fact, he pretty much got me through the year."

As the graduates return to their seats, diplomas in hand, the headmaster, Dr. Ryan, announces he will release a white dove to commemorate the loss of Mary Loverwest. A man walks onto the stage and folds the white bird into Dr. Ryan's hands. Dr. Ryan then holds it for one moment, lifts it up, and pushes it while its wings open. The bird seems flustered, panicky, and jerks around over the audience, until it senses the break in the trees and goes to the blue. It soars in a wild, natural arc.

Dr. Ryan slowly returns to the podium and leans to the mike. "It is my distinct pleasure to congratulate the graduating class."

Caps fly into the air, and seniors take off down the hill to jump in the lake, as per tradition. It's over.

One by one the guys stand up, swipe gravel from their pants, and leave the roof, uttering a barely audible "peace" as they make their way down the ladder. Chase wonders where the dove will end up.

Departures take place over the next few days, and this staggering makes for a disjointed collective good-bye. Chase is crossing the field near the art studios, having just seen off

Greg in his granddad's taupe Caddy, which his parents borrowed to come get him, and here comes Parker from the art rooms. She's carrying two canvases that are bound with twine, facing each other, the wood frame visible on the outsides.

"Park!"

She blinks at him, not sure who this crewcut guy is. "Oh my God, Chase?"

He rubs his bristles, grinning. "All gone."

She looks at him with that ten-year-old expression of wide-eyed frankness. "I don't know what to say."

He can tell she's talking about his haircut, and about everything else that has happened, too. She wears a tight Pink Floyd T-shirt and jeans. Behind her, white moths touch down and lift off the Scotch broom blooming butter yellow against the clapboard side of the art barn. It shouldn't be her burden to say anything at all.

"So what are your plans this summer?" he asks.

She shakes her head. Shifts the paintings on her hips, reluctantly bemused. "I don't know, Chase. What are you doing?"

"My dad's got me working at the harbor, and caddying at the club."

"Sounds pretty typical."

"At least I'll be working, not playing. And if I get two weeks off at the end and make enough cash, I'm going to

270

travel on my own, maybe even get up north."

"Your dad's going to go for that?"

"I hope so. I'm going to build a strong case. I just think he'll eventually get it."

"Is shaving your head a bargaining chip?"

He shrugs.

"I wish you well on your little Kerouac plan. Good luck."

"I've got a question. Will you be home in August?"

"I might be. And I might not."

"Well, I'm coming anyway," he says without hesitation.

She starts to walk off, and he holds up the letter. "Wait a sec. This is for you."

She takes it, smiling reluctantly, but when he reaches for her, she moves back.

Walks backward, waving in a way that means for him to stay where he is, she doesn't want a hug.

"Bye!" she calls, and then turns away from him.

"Bye."

He watches her hair shimmer darkly down her back as she crosses the Technicolor field, those long skinny legs making deep strides to wherever it is she wants to go. He wonders what the paintings look like, since only a bit of paint has bled through to their backsides. They might be two self-portraits, in silent and clandestine consultation.

* * *

When Parker arrives home in two days, she'll leave her bags and boxes in the driveway to walk around, inside and out, and make sure it's the same home she left. The same skylight letting in the same Canadian sun. The same cat, Raisin, cuddled under an afghan. The same mother and father, with the same love for her. Finn, the same cool customer. Outside, the crazy jumble they call a garden grows around the cedar-shingled house: jalapeño entwined with honeysuckle, wild strawberries next to bamboo, mint and roses and tomatoes. The smell of cornbread cooking in the kitchen profoundly transports her from Being Away to Being Back.

She'll find Blue, at the coffee shop where he's working. The rings on his hands—skulls and crosses and bats—blink as he grinds beans. His new best friend, Caleb, a skinny guy so tall he bends his spine to fit better in rooms, wears a torn Cure T-shirt and a porkpie hat, loiters at the café, and drinks his coffee black. Blue doesn't belong to Parker anymore.

But her real destination her first afternoon home, the star on her map of returning, is someone else. She goes to his house, where his older brother and his friends are skating the ramp they built, Gorillaz thumping from a radio. They tell her he's mowing the Martins' field.

So she walks over there, smiling, breathing in rich summer, the breeze almost gilding her with pollen. She ties her black tank top in a knot, her cut-off black jean skirt hanging low on her hips, and she slips off her flip-flops and walks barefoot. Golden sky, emerald meadows. The place where she's grown up shimmers around her and through her.

In the distance, a yellow cloud of dust blooms after the tractor. *We don't get a million chances.* Sun shines off Peter's hair and his long, wet arms. She smiles; he's about to turn, he's about to see her coming to him.

Don't miss next semester:

OFF CAMPUS:
AN UPPER CLASS NOVEL

The new Wellington year begins. The school is cracked open like an egg. BMWs and Volvos and Land Rovers are parked on the lawns in front of dorms, their back doors lifted to a tumble of freshly washed linens and milk crates of books and computers and Mark Cross duffels. Parents make polite hellos to each other as they pass in the stone halls, and they make sad good-byes to their kids.

"What's up, playa?" some kid in madras shorts says.

"Chilling. How you been?" The two guys slap hands, smile slyly as if this is the year they're going to get over.

"Yee *ha*," growls Brenda Fahey at the top of her lungs from the commons. She's a stout, tough girl from Michigan, a softball legend, and her friends now flock to her like puppies to a master, all of them in Umbros and jog

1

bras under college T-shirts.

Parker, Nikki, Noah, and Greg got here yesterday and are now enjoying what feels like the last day of summer on Parker's great-aunt's quilt on Rooster Hill overlooking Dory Lake. The day is just too plump and golden, like a fruit about to burst, to ever be repeated this September. Most returning students are already here, straggling in from their hometowns, pinning up tapestries in new rooms, checking out views, sniffing the air for trouble or promise. They're connecting one by one.

And today new students arrive. The campus is electrified, as if waiting to see what mother brings home from the hospital.

"I'm glad we don't have to go through that again." Parker points her long, slender hand, Tibetan beads hanging from her ivory wrist, to new students on their way down to the picnic.

"Oh my *God*," Nikki agrees. "I pity them. I mean, look at that little boy in glasses over there by himself. He looks *eight*. Did we stick out like that?"

"Hell, yes," Parker says easily.

For returning students, orientation blows air through stale halls. A new crop means another chance at a best friend, a bigger crew, a new crush, a better hook-up. The returning students feel the hierarchy of the school shifting, like walking over cracked tiles on an old floor. New cliques take over prime cafeteria tables, and the kids who swung from their tighty-whiteys on the flagpole last year turn into this fall's monster-hazers. *The meek shall inherit the school.* The unofficial understudies of the star-seniors who graduated last year come out on the stage now, blinking in the pure, stark spotlight.

Summer gossip crystallizes into legend. *Did you hear about Fielding getting kicked out of Windridge for hooking up with a camper? Dude, what about Jill Lassiter? She's not coming back. She wrecked her mom's Audi, crashed into Shinnecock's gazebo. Her parents chucked her in rehab just so they wouldn't get thrown out of the club. Martin Helbridge's mom committed suicide; he found her in the garden shed. This uncle took him to Cairo, and he's still there.*

Greg Jenson and Noah Ashton sprawl on the quilt, their big bodies incongruous to the country-plaid and floral squares of fabric. All afternoon they've been studying the Facebook, which arrived in mailboxes like an early Christmas gift.

"Have we identified her yet?" Greg points to a Lower-form girl from San Sebastian, Spain.

"Roger that. False alarm. She must have Photoshopped herself."

"You guys are evil sometimes," Parker says lazily.

She's lying back, one hand shielding her face from the sun. A sliver of stomach shows between her worn olive

Carharts and CBGB T-shirt, and Nikki catches the guys looking. Noah even shakes his head. Nikki figures they're both thinking the same thing. *Fuckin' A, Chase really blew it.*

"Yo, who's *that*?" Greg points to a blonde from La Jolla on the next page.

"You mean Delia?" Nikki adjusts her white tank top and pulls down her jean shorts.

"You know her?" Noah asks.

"Yeah, I met her when I was out there with Seth. She's a friend of his sister's."

"Shit, hook a brother up." Greg rips out a few blades of grass and tosses them in Nikki's direction.

"Not sure she goes for meatheads." Nikki winks at Greg, who's wearing his varsity football T-shirt. "Especially ones with fight scars."

Everyone laughs. Greg has four cuts on his neck, like a claw mark, from a fight he got into at a baseball game in his park in Brooklyn a week ago. He'd been drinking, not much, but everyone knows Greg cannot hold even a thimble of liquor.

"All right, all right, whatever," he says, rolling his eyes.

"But if I *do* hook you up, you better return the favor," Nikki kids him.

"You on the prowl, Nik?" Noah smirks.

She's known this would come up. But everything that happened with Seth last week is too fresh and too precious to talk about with these guys. She proceeds with bravado, and checks out her nails: "Maybe." Nikki's surprised at herself, because she's actually proud to belong to Seth exclusively. But some part of her doesn't want to be cut out of the picture here.

"How about you, Park?" Noah asks.

"Off. Officially," Parker deadpans.

Nikki laughs.

"It's not that funny." Parker stares at Nikki.

"I know, sorry, it's just how you said it."